I0783921

# THE RAMBLING MAN

# THE RAMBLING MAN

GABE REAUME

THE RAMBLING MAN Copyright ©2025 by Gabe Reaume.

All rights reserved. Printed in the United States of America. No part of this book may be used or reproduced in any form without written permission except in the case of brief quotations embodied in critical articles and reviews.

Library of Congress Cataloging-in-Publication Data: TXu 2-477-541

First Edition

Book cover and Book interior designed by Glen M. Edelstein

979-8-9888577-2-3  (Trade Paperback)
979-8-9888577-3-0 (Ebook)
979-8-9888577-4-7 (Audiobook)

# THE RAMBLING MAN

# CHAPTER ONE

Looking serious, a lumbering old man shook his head as he eyed the teenaged cashier behind the counter. "You again?" Kenneth Love asked.

"I don't want any trouble, sir. I just want your tab paid," Merene Cory said.

"Well, good land, is that all?" His laugh lingered for a while and then sputtered out with a wheeze and a cough as he gasped to regain his composure, as the elderly often did when they got excited.

He swayed from side to side as he moved around the store, looking like some cowboy wearing spurs in an old-timey Western movie, not because he wanted to but because he had had both hips replaced a few years ago. Raising cattle and farming were hell on the body, especially on the joints.

The Glastonbury Market was a relic of a bygone era where customers could still keep a tab and pay monthly. Once upon a time, it was the company store for the Glastonbury Mining Company. It wasn't really a grocery store, but it was definitely a little more than a run-of-the-mill gas station and convenience store, the only retail establishment Novinger, Missouri, had to offer. It likely would stay in business forever, since it saved the straggling survivors of the long-decrepit coal mining town from driving to the "big" city of Kirksville, a hilly fifteen minutes east along State Highway 6.

Old-timers like Kenneth Love poked in regularly for simple human interaction; his kids and grandkids had long since departed for Kirksville or Columbia or Saint Louis or Kansas City. The relatively few younger people of working age in Novinger trekked to the colossal pig farms in Milan, pronounced not like the city in Italy but rather "My Lynn." Workers drove thirty minutes west on Highway 6 if they weren't employed by the hotels, restaurants, or other marks of civilization near Truman State University in Kirksville.

Merene knew exactly what he would get. It was a Monday; he'd be in for a loaf of square-top sandwich wheat bread and a jar of smooth peanut butter. She could set a clock by his routine.

She had a plastic knife ready for him to spread the peanut butter on the bread, which he would fold in half. His coffee, black and boiling hot, was waiting for him at the counter.

"Never gets old," he said. He slurped the coffee then chewed the juicy concoction he had drowned in the cup.

A customer wearing greasy coveralls walked in, jingling the bell on the door as it swung open. He rummaged through the aisles and made his way to the counter.

"A ham-factory man," Kenneth said. "You smell 'em before you see 'em."

The cologne the man wore couldn't hide the aroma of cured meat, which, among bodily odors, probably wasn't the worst thing out there.

Amid the hustle and bustle of the morning rush, Merene was looking forward to hearing Kenneth call her name. He was firmly set in his octogenarian ways, and his deep voice made her ears tingle when he said her real name, which so few people did.

"Merene."

He pronounced it correctly, a phonetic combination of "May" and "Serene" concocted by a young mother who thought her daughter's eyes were as serene as the sea, la mer in French, which had been her favorite subject in high school. Less than a finger counting's worth of people actually called her by her real name.

Merene had watched Kenneth do this song and dance a thousand times before, breaking out his checkbook to pay his monthly grocery, gas, and propane bill to the Glastonbury Company, which had long since dropped the "Mining" from its name.

"Kenneth, you messed up already," Merene said.

"Do what?"

She was used to his reply. He didn't offer a solitary "what;" it was always prefaced by a "do." Old men were predictable.

"The 'pay to the order' part should be 'Merene Cory,' not Glastonbury Company," she said.

It was their running joke. She loved to see him smile.

Kenneth was an eye-smiler, the sort of person whose goodness couldn't be faked. Eye-smilers were the honest-to-goodness salt of the earth. Plenty of people peeled their lips up at the corners to show off their teeth, trying to hide the fact that they were no good or liars or had all sorts of undesirable qualities.

"Have you been talkin' to Sharyn? She seems to think I need to pay her too."

Sharyn was Kenneth's wife. A country woman, she was quiet and reserved and didn't talk much. She didn't need to, since Kenneth talked enough for the both of them. They were newlyweds, having only been married twenty-something years. Kenneth's first wife had passed from complications of unchecked diabetes. Sharyn had married an older man as a teenager and divorced at some point long ago.

The couple were stalwarts in the Novinger United Methodist Church, where Merene had met them as a child during vacation Bible school, which was the closest thing to summer camp any kid in Novinger ever got. Merene and the Loves ate dinner, which was the Midwest term for a big lunch, after church every Sunday. "Supper" was the proper term for an evening meal. They piled onto the bench seat of Kenneth's old but well-maintained green Chevy truck for the ride to the City, a greasy spoon in Kirksville located right where US 63 met Highway 6 as Highway 6 bounded west into the flyover country where Novinger stood.

"Dinner was good yesterday," Merene said. "Half the company was terrible, though. The other half was lovely."

"How dare you talk about Sharyn like that. She's not even here to defend her honor!" Kenneth said.

"She was the lovely part, sir."

"Ain't that the truth! I think I'll order something different than my usual pork tenderloin sandwich next week. Doctor in Kirksville wants me to watch my figure and my blood sugar. Sharyn's watching what I eat like a hawk."

"You will not," Merene said. "Who are you kidding? You've eaten the same thing twice as long as I've been alive."

"True. And I clean the plate every time!"

"Good morning, Lovel," a customer said to Kenneth. "How you feelin'?"

In his younger days, Kenneth had acquired the nickname Lovel, which was a mishmash of his last name, Love, and "level," like the tool used for carpentry. Levels had little tubes with liquid and a bubble in the middle. His round belly was the bubble in the middle.

"Movin' a little slower these days but still just as pretty as can be," Kenneth said. He offered the man a hearty handshake and backslap.

For some odd reason, the A in his signature—"Kenneth A. Love"—struck Merene that day. She realized she didn't know what it meant.

"Kenneth, what does the A stand for?"

He looked up from his focused strain over the production of neat penmanship. His thick, sausage-like fingers made the pen look like a toothpick in his hands. "Well, well, well. What's it to ya, young lady?"

Merene didn't reply, hoping the strength of silence alone would volunteer an answer.

According to the time clock ticking in her head, she had less than a couple of minutes before the stray ice cubes that made their way to the floor from customers who filled their morning soft drinks in too much of a hurry melted into a puddle, creating a slip hazard. She would have to venture out from behind the counter to wipe them up and dry the floor before Barnabas Hassan made his morning round. He was older than the hills and surely couldn't afford to pay the price of a slip and fall.

"I bet you a Coke you can't guess it. A real Coke, not one of those silver-can Cokes for women and children," he said. "Sharyn has me drinking women's Cokes without the sugar. It just ain't the same."

Merene rang up the cost of the drink on the register. Challenge accepted. "Adam," she said.

"No."

"Eve?"

Kenneth closed his eyes and shook his head, trying his best to look gruff. He really liked that quip, Merene could tell.

"Did you not learn in school 'Eve' doesn't begin with the letter A?"

"Abel."

"No."

"Abraham."

He shook his head.

"Andrew."

He shook again.

"Alexander."

And again.

Kenneth continued to shake his head even before Merene had offered another name.

"Keep trying, but I win this time," he said. He popped the tab of his liquid victory celebration and took a slow sip as the fizz sizzled. "Refreshing."

"Give me a hint, Kenneth."

"Cheaters never prosper. How's that?" His sparkling blue eyes twinkled. "Flahr."

"Did you say 'flower'? You can't be serious. Your parents named you after a plant?"

"That's for me to know and you to find out. Would I lie to you?"

"Azalea."

Kenneth choked on his Coke, staining the collar of his pearl-snap shirt that was likely older than Merene by at least a decade.

"Aster. Alyssum. Amaryllis?"

During the guessing game, a white fox terrier with a black spot on his head bounded into the store, the telltale sign its owner, the aged Barnabas Hassan, wouldn't be far behind.

"Merene, the A is for annoying," said Sharyn, who had let in the dog, Diz, when she'd opened the door to come inside.

"Amen!" Merene said.

Merene was convinced that Diz actually understood English. He nodded his head and made facial expressions like a person did when they talked. The little dog must have heard "flour." He bounded back a few aisles, where he sat with his head and nose angled to point directly at a five-pound bag of flour—the baking kind—sitting on a shelf.

Merene had come out from behind the counter to clean up the ice cube puddles.

"You have one last guess, sweet Merene," Kenneth said.

"You have one last sip, Mr. Love," Sharyn said. She saw he had snuck a real sugar Coke when she wasn't watching.

"One more hint?" Merene asked. She didn't care about the cost of the Coke. She knew Kenneth wouldn't make her pay for it. It was the principle of the matter. She wanted to win.

"Excalibur," he said.

"Ex-what? For goodness sakes, Kenneth. Isn't that a cigar brand?"

"How would you know that?" he asked.

A teenaged boy wearing running shorts and a faded gray T-shirt that said "Army" in block letters patiently held the door for an older man as he inched cautiously inside.

"Peaches," Kenneth said to the young man. "How can someone who runs every day all over Adair County have legs so pale? What are you runnin' from?"

"I think my legs are handsome, Kenneth," Peaches said. "They're not pale. They just shine brightly."

"Shine brightly?" Merene and Sharyn parroted him in unison. They burst into laughter.

"Why the army?" Kenneth asked. He turned his head halfway to Merene. "We all know you're a lover, not a fighter."

"You got that right. I am a lover." Peaches winked at Merene and smacked his lips to make a kissing sound. "Here's how I see it, Kenneth. The army is the world's largest coed running club. They run every single day, sometimes for no apparent reason. I join up with them and wear an army uniform for a couple of years, they'll pay for me to go to college."

"Arthur. Kenneth's father's name was Arthur," Barnabas Hassan said, his voice not much above a whisper.

"You know, like King Arthur flour? Or King Arthur in that Disney movie that came out a couple of years ago, The Sword in the Stone?" Kenneth said.

Sharyn gave a hearty harumph. "Kenneth, that movie came out in the early sixties. Almost forty years ago!"

"Well, pardon me," Kenneth said. "I'm still recovering from the emotional trauma of Y2K last year. It seems to have affected my memory."

"Kenneth, you wouldn't know how to turn a computer on if someone pointed a gun to your head," Merene said.

"You wouldn't either. The gun would make you nervous!" He wheezed at his joke as the women laughed.

Merene poured another hot black coffee. "Good morning, Barnabas Hassan."

Hassan, in northeast Missouri (pronounced "Mizz-urr-uh") parlance, sounded like "Hazz-in."

"Thank you kindly, Merene," Barnabas said.

Barnabas was also a natural eye-smiler. When he spoke, which wasn't often, others' worries, fears, and uncertainties seemed to disappear. He might as well have been one of the saints on those prayer cards Catholics carried. The only thing he was missing was a halo floating above his head.

"Arthur Love was a good man," Barnabas said, reminiscing.

"Yes, he was," Kenneth said.

Merene noticed Kenneth brushing an unexpected tear from his eye. And she saw Diz wipe at his eye with a paw, as if he, too, had let a sudden drop of emotion leak forth.

What a ham. That dog really was something else.

# CHAPTER TWO

---

"Ma'am?" a customer said to Merene. "Can you tell me where the Coal Miners' Museum is?"

He was wearing flip-flops and swim trunks, was sunburnt, and had to be from out of town— maybe from Saint Louis, judging by the Cardinals ball cap on his head.

"Came to stay at Thousand Hills State Park?"

"Yes. It's wonderful out here! The hills and the lake and the fresh country air. The cabins are really nice. We even went caving. Saw those petroglyphs Native Americans scratched on the walls thousands of years ago. The caves were amazing, but, except in one of the deepest spots, it stunk like something had died."

Diz growled.

"You're really lucky to live so close to all of this. I'm dreading having to head back to Saint Louis soon."

Merene was glad the visitor had had a good time but found his gushing about the area overdone. No one in Novinger could afford camping in the cabins at the state park. Then again, no one in Novinger would pay to camp in their own backyard.

"The museum isn't much—just a metal barn with some pictures and a tabletop model of a mine. There's a logbook with the names of miners past. Some of my relatives are in it," Merene said.

"Is it worth visiting?" the man asked. "How long have the mines been closed? Hate to be mean, but this town looks like it's been dead for years."

"I'll let you decide that. You probably don't have anything like it in Saint Louis, if I had to guess. You're just a few blocks away, if they're open today."

Barnabas introduced himself to the stranger and offered his hand. "My name is Barnabas Hassan," he said. "Welcome to Novinger. We're proud of our little town."

"You should be!" the man said. "It's like Mayberry!"

"I'll take you to the Coal Miners' Museum. Years and years ago, I used to run the Glastonbury Mining Company. The company founder, J. O. Armati, came from Glastonbury, England. We closed the mines for good in the 1960s. It's been hard to keep people here since then. They have to go to the big cities to find decent jobs."

"I'll drive you, Barnabas," Sharyn said.

Merene chimed in. "When you see the logbook, many of the family names that fill it—the Corys and the McKims and the Williams and the Cimas and Baiottos—they're still around here." She stepped out from behind the counter to speak for a moment. "Don't forget to eat something this morning, Barnabas."

Merene had to remind him sometimes. He ate like a bird and lived by himself with Diz, his faithful fox terrier, to keep him company. Diz had to be old like Barnabas, but he was as playful and spry as a puppy. No one remembered a time in Novinger without Barnabas or Diz.

"You look great for your age, sir," the newcomer said, taking the old man's arm to steady him. "Full head of hair. Dark too!" The stranger lifted the ball cap from his head, revealing his baldness. "I'm jealous!"

Barnabas took careful, measured baby steps, as the elderly often did. He liked to pace with his left hand balled into a fist behind his back. With head lowered, he would place his right index and middle fingers on his forehead while resting his thumb on his cheek, deep in thought. His eyes were piercing and lucid.

"Thank you kindly, Merene," he said. "I'll see you this afternoon."

Barnabas Hassan had employed generations of Cory men when the mines were active. Now he employed two Cory women, Merene and her mother, Teresa, who was aptly nicknamed Mother Teresa, to run the Glastonbury Market and look after his rent houses. He literally owned half the town. Most of his renters couldn't afford to pay, which didn't seem to bother the man at all. Merene delivered Mr. Hassan's mail to him after school.

Merene's mother walked in to relieve her daughter from the ball and chain of the cash register.

"I bet you'll have some books waiting for you," Merene said.

A bibliophile, Barnabas received dusty old tomes from around the world: the United Kingdom, Greece, Italy, Israel, the Vatican. He had traveled the world over and had letters from his acquaintances to prove it.

Barnabas nodded at Merene's comment. "Shall we?" he said to the man as they made their way to the door. "Merene, have a wonderful day. You, too, Teresa. And Kenneth, you behave."

Peaches had slipped out without anyone noticing.

The warmth that always radiated from Barnabas made Merene believe she was destined to be so much more than the poor daughter of a single mother, doomed to work for eternity in a no-horse town's convenience store. Other than Merene, Barnabas was the only other person in Novinger who possessed a skin tone a shade darker than snow-white. Hers was a credit to the medical-student father she would never know.

# CHAPTER THREE

The out-of-towner froze for a moment. The Coal Miners' Museum, caked in a thin veneer of dust, was a walk-in time capsule with a concrete floor. Its neon lights buzzed as they warmed up and slowly illuminated the simple building, not much bigger than an oversized garage and supported by metal poles.

"Please sign the visitors' log," Barnabas said.

The man found that the last guest entry was some six months ago. He cautiously scratched out letters on brittle, yellowed paper. He wrote "Saint Louis, Missouri," under a column labeled "From" to the right of his name.

Sharyn momentarily disappeared into a back room then returned with a broom and dustpan. "This place is filthy. Certainly not fit for company. We apologize for the mess."

"Don't worry about it, ma'am. It's fine," the man said.

"A man works from sun to sun," Sharyn said. "A woman's work is never done."

Swift flits of the broom launched dust clouds airborne. The morning sunlight pierced through the particles like a kaleidoscope.

"Glastonbury," the man said, reading from a monument sign in a dated picture of the Glastonbury Mine in an album. "Why Glastonbury?"

Barnabas smiled like a schoolchild who had patiently waited to be called upon. "The company that opened the mines was from Glastonbury, England."

The man flipped through the album. "What are these shrubs? They're in almost every picture."

Barnabas spoke up again. "They're Glastonbury hawthorns, thorny little trees native to England, so I'm told. Almost all of the miners and their families lived in houses owned by the company, all of which had Glastonbury hawthorns planted in the front yard."

"That is so neat," the man said. "Local lore."

"That's not the half of it," Sharyn chimed in as she rested her hand and chin on top of the broom handle. "Our Glastonbury hawthorns here in Novinger bloom on Christmas Day and then again six months later. I can't remember a Christmas when the hawthorns didn't bloom, even when there's snow on the ground."

The man continued to stroll through the museum with his hands tucked behind his back. He found a stack of old newspapers, carefully preserved under stiff plastic sleeves.

"Olive Wood Gymnasium for the Children of Farmers and Coal Miners," read a headline. Underneath was a faded picture of a sturdy, round-faced man with Benjamin Franklin spectacles, flanked closely by a woman. Behind them were lines of people three rows deep.

"What's this?"

"That's our pride and joy. Our schoolhouse. The community built it brick by brick. The man and woman at the front are Arthur and Clara Love," Barnabas said.

"My husband's parents. Arthur was the school board president," Sharyn said. "In those days, the school board president was the principal."

The man read the fragments of the article that weren't too faded to decipher. "'Visitors marvel at the gymnasium floor, almost too pretty to walk on. It's made of olive wood. Three times as hard as oak and naturally moisture resistant, it won't warp or buckle. It was laid by Mr. Barnabas Hassan, the finest carpenter since our Lord walked the earth.'"

"We were young and foolish then," Barnabas said. "Arthur and I figured that if Thomas Jefferson designed and built Monticello by himself, we could build a schoolhouse. We read a few books about architecture. Arthur drafted the blueprints and specifications and modified them slightly from building plans bought from a mail-order Sears & Roebuck catalog. The Glastonbury Company furnished the building materials."

"Is the school still standing?"

"Yes," Barnabas said.

The man continued thumbing through the archive.

"$500 Pie," another newspaper headline read.

"The school board had to raise money to pay the bills in the old days. We held a roast beef supper in the fall and a pie supper in the spring," Barnabas said.

"It says here you bought a record-setting, five-hundred-dollar mincemeat pie, Mr. Hassan," the man said.

"I suppose I did. We all buy things on impulse from time to time."

Sharyn handed a cup of black tea to Barnabas. Barnabas sipped as Sharyn returned to tidying up.

The final article, from 1962, showed a large bold headline: "Great Glastonbury Fire."

Pictures below the gaudy, oversized type showed the mine entrance billowing black smoke like a freight train. Other pictures showed seams in the ground, cracked and smoking.

"Is this what closed the mines for good?" the man asked.

Barnabas nodded.

The man read a portion of the article out loud. "'A miner, who wished to remain anonymous, stated the following:

"I saw a man without eyes start the fire. Yes! He had holes in his head where eyes should have been. He had a putrid, rotting smell, unlike anything I've ever experienced. I heard another man's voice scream, 'Justice! Justice!' I passed out. Someone carried me to safety.'"

Diz growled.

The visitor bit his lip. "That's exactly the way I would describe what I smelled when I was in the caves by the state park. It was worse than death, if you can imagine that."

After several minutes more of rummaging through memorabilia, the visitor shook hands with Barnabas and Sharyn and left.

"Gestas?" Sharyn asked. "He can't possibly be back again?"

Diz barked and growled. Barnabas hung his head.

# CHAPTER FOUR

——————

"I better get back to Seven Hills Way," Kenneth said. "Sharyn works me pretty hard."

Kenneth and Sharyn lived on their farm, Seven Hills Way, a few miles outside of Novinger, along the Chariton River bottoms.

"I'm a bottom-feeder," Kenneth always said when asked what he did for a living. "A river-bottom farmer. Farmers feed people. Ya get it?"

The house he was raised in, as plain as oatmeal without brown sugar, stood next to the house he built when he got married at the ripe old age of eighteen. His childhood home was spare—one room with a small kitchen, built of sturdy blocks, one at a time, by his father and mother. His grandparents were pioneers from out east before they settled and built a log cabin, which burned down at some point long ago. Kenneth and Sharyn, on hands and knees, had planted a huge vegetable garden out back. They stuck annual flowers wherever cracks, crevices, and daylight allowed around the house. The Seven Hills Way homestead was like something from the cover of a long-forgotten Saturday Evening Post.

After he visited Merene and Mother Teresa at the Glastonbury Market for coffee and chitchat, it was time for him to "head to the office." As old men did, he laughed the loudest at his own corny jokes. In beaten-up, patched-twice-over bib overalls, he set off to whatever task the day might bring.

"Variety is the spice of life," Kenneth said, repeating the often-repeated phrase. "That makes farmers like me spicy."

Nostalgic, Kenneth thought of his father as he caught sight of the King Arthur flour on the shelves while heading for the door. It made him very proud to think that wheat he grew might be inside one of those paper bags, waiting to nourish.

Arthur had been a farmer because he had to be, not because he wanted to be. His heart and mind were with studying and teaching. Arthur and his wife, Clara, were godly people that folks in Novinger had looked up to. Like any father, Arthur had hoped his son would take after him and maybe study at the college in Kirksville. But Kenneth was born with a toe in the soil. School wasn't for him. Farming would be his life's work.

"They only let me graduate, I think, because Dad was on the school board," Kenneth had told Merene one time. "I hated school and couldn't wait to be outside every day." In the springtime, he became giddy like a kid on Christmas morning. He couldn't wait to get out into the fields to get them ready for planting. The first step in the process was to pick out rocks that had come to the surface of the fields after hiding under winter snow.

Merene had started her working career as a grade-school rock-spotter sitting on Kenneth's lap while he drove the tractor.

"What's this one worth?" she would ask as she picked the rock out of the soil and piled it in the bucket.

"We'll settle up back at the barn," Kenneth would say. He paid his child laborer in candy and Cokes.

Free from rocky obstructions, Kenneth would plow and disc and cultivate until it was the right time to inject seeds of corn, soybeans, wheat, oats, and hay into the earth for safekeeping. Once he had done his part, it was up to God to do the rest.

After school, Merene brought Barnabas and Kenneth and Sharyn their mail, which was delivered, like all the rest of Novinger's, to the market for people to pick up at their leisure.

Barnabas's house was not much bigger than the one Kenneth had grown up in. It was close to the entrance of the long-dormant, deep-shaft coal mine that the Glastonbury Mining Company had operated for decades. The entrance to the cavernous bore had been sealed with a cluster of rocks and a large flat stone that probably weighed a few tons, reminiscent of something the Biblical angel rolled away after the resurrection of Christ.

# CHAPTER FIVE

---

"For God's sake, Mom. I washed and folded your clothes. Can you at least put them away?" Merene didn't expect a response. "And we don't have any clean bowls because I know they're all dirty in your bedroom."

"I'm sorry, baby. I know."

A little later, Teresa carried to the kitchen sink half a dozen bowls with spoons glued to the sides by dried cereal and funky milk in various stages of rot and decay.

"Thanks, I guess."

"Merene, I don't know what I'd do without you."

"Dishes, maybe?"

They both laughed.

Teresa kissed Merene on the cheek. Merene turned on the hot water, and bubbles multiplied exponentially as the stinky dishes soaked.

Sadly, the child was the parent in their household.

Teresa had struggled with a number of demons, namely depression and addiction. Like many, she used a variety of chemicals to self-medicate. For as long as she could remember, Merene had made sure her mother took her antidepressants as she was supposed to. She watched her closely, calling her out when she quit taking her meds, a never-ending job.

Like her daughter, Teresa had dreamed of becoming a doctor. She was once well on her way to seeing her dream come true. She graduated from Truman State University in Kirksville, majoring in biology. She had applied to Kirksville College of Osteopathic Medicine, and was accepted. Teresa was randomly assigned a guide for a campus tour, a second-year medical student named Christian Balthazar.

It was, as they said, love at first sight.

"I'm Christian," he said, extending his hand to the young woman.

"So am I," Teresa said, mistakenly hearing that he was a Christian. "United Methodist."

"My name is Christian," he said, trying again.

"Teresa. Where are you from?"

She tried not to stare at his wavy black hair and green eyes, traits they both shared. She wondered if his caramel-toned skin was as sweet as it looked.

The young Creole smiled. "Louisiana," he said. "Not Louisiana, Missouri. Louisiana as in, I'm from near New Orleans. How about you? Where are you from?"

"You wouldn't know it if I told you."

"How do you know that? I might."

"I'm from a small nothing town west of here called Novinger."

The campus tour was a dizzying flurry of flirtation. At its conclusion, Chrisian offered Teresa his number.

"You can call me anytime if you have questions about medical school, or if you want to talk. About anything."

He shook her hand when they parted, holding back the urge to kiss her. She resisted the same urge.

They soon became inseparable.

"Novinger isn't nearly as bad as you say it is," Christian told Teresa as he sat next to her in a pew at the Novinger United Methodist Church, not long after they first met. "These people love me, even though I'm Catholic!"

"Balthazar," Barnabas Hassan said, repeating the young man's last name. Christian had introduced himself as a guest of Teresa Cory's to rowdy applause in the fellowship hall, where people congregated for coffee and cookies after the Sunday service had concluded. "Balthazar was one of the Three Wise Men who came to see the baby Jesus."

Kenneth listened to Barnabas. "Wise Guy, then," he said. "Your name from now on is Wise Guy. It suits you."

Teresa piped up. "I'm jealous, Kenneth. I've known you my entire life and I don't get a nickname?"

Kenneth's brow furled. He looked directly at Christian as he spoke. "Mrs. Wise Guy."

Teresa blushed.

With the way Christian and Teresa looked at each other, everybody knew they would marry. It was just a matter of time.

One evening, Teresa and Christian drove from their apartment in Kirksville to eat and play cards and dominoes at Seven Hills Way with Kenneth and Sharyn until the wee hours of the following morning.

"Sir," Christian said to Kenneth, "can I talk to you?"

Teresa was in the bathroom. They were driving back to Kirksville in a minute or two.

"Who is 'sir'?" Kenneth asked.

"I love her, Kenneth. I absolutely love her! I figured I needed your blessing before I asked. You're the closest thing to a father she has."

He opened a small ring box he had been hiding in his back pocket.

"Well, you've got my blessing, young man," Kenneth said. He locked Christian up in a bear hug so tight it was a little uncomfortable for the doctor-in-training.

The couple eloped, and Teresa became pregnant. She was accepted to medical school, set to attend the following year. Their life and future together would be perfect.

Until it wasn't.

Christian had volunteered for a medical mission in West Africa. The opportunity to help those ravaged by disease and conflict inspired him. He wouldn't have to learn the language. While he grew up embarrassed of his thick Louisiana Creole accent and the slang French he spoke at home before learning English, it would be put to good use comforting the native French speakers in desperate need of medical attention across the ocean.

His pregnant wife couldn't go with him. It was a few short weeks apart, he told her. Someday they would heal the needy together across the world. He'd be back well before the baby came.

"Please," Christian begged Teresa. "I don't know that there's anything I've wanted more. Anything except you." He kissed her forehead, and she sighed.

"Okay," she said. "But I'll be a worrying mess until you come back."

Reluctantly, Teresa let him go, a decision she would regret for the rest of her life.

It was Barnabas who received the first word of Christian's death. Armed rebels had attacked the refugee camp where he was providing vaccinations. They came to steal kids to make them into child soldiers or worse. Christian Balthazar stood tall, shielding frightened villagers with his body until guerrilla bullets ensured he would stand no more.

His daughter would be born half a world away a few months later. Baby Merene was given her mother's maiden name, which Teresa had kept after she married. Christian's last name was too painful of a reminder to live with.

Teresa never made it to medical school. Caring for her baby and working at the Glastonbury Market was all she could handle. The hard times came and went with Teresa's mental illness. If it weren't for Kenneth and Sharyn and Barnabas, Merene would have ended up in the state foster care system.

The worst hard time was when Merene was twelve years old. Teresa had what psychiatrists would call a major depressive episode. She watched TV for weeks on the couch, listlessly. Merene had to dress and feed her mother like she was a child.

"You stink," Merene said. "I'm sick of it."

She brought a big popcorn bowl and washed her mother's hair on the couch because she wouldn't get up and shower herself. Teresa was like a toy with batteries that were dying. She moved and made noise and blinked, but she was fading. Mental illness be damned to hell, Merene thought. It wasn't her mother's fault she was crazy. Deep down, she was a really good person. Teresa was hospitalized for a few weeks.

At times, usually in the night, the wolves in Teresa's head stalked her and howled and reminded her how she was stuck in the middle of nowhere and that she was a nobody. Most times she could keep the wolves at bay by thinking about Merene, her hope in the flesh.

# CHAPTER SIX

A few months later, in the spring of her junior year, Merene found herself living with Kenneth and Sharyn when her mother managed to acquire the lowest of lowlifes as a live-in.

"I can't understand what the hell she sees in him. Surely being single is better than having a boyfriend who prides himself on being called Dipshit," Merene said to Sharyn as they sat at the kitchen table after she brought the mail. They were planning on Peaches joining them for supper. Sharyn made the best beans and hot skillet cornbread around. In the epic war of men versus women, Kenneth and Peaches would team up against Merene and Sharyn in games of dominoes or cards for hours. It was the highlight of the week. Kenneth was out in the fields but had mentioned he wanted the three of them to take a drive before Peaches came by.

Teresa's boyfriend, Dalton Reese, had only one redeeming quality. Ruddy, muscular, and auburn-haired, he was certainly attractive.

"She's lonely, young 'un," Sharyn said. "Loneliness does bad things to good people."

"I know, but he's loud and crude and disgusting and dumb. He doesn't even say hello when he answers the phone. He screams 'Dipshit' as loud as possible and laughs. It's not funny the first time you hear it, much less the hundred and first."

Merene had told her mother she was going to move out if she didn't kick Dipshit out of the house. The second-to-last straw came when Merene found a pair of Teresa's underwear wedged under a couch cushion.

"I'm sorry," Teresa said. "It must have fallen out when I was folding laundry."

"Since when have you folded laundry? I've done it for both of us since grade school!" Merene shouted.

Merene shuddered to think that her pretty and smart mother had hooked up with Dipshit on the couch they shared.

Teresa had gained a lot of weight from a recent change in medication. She had been steady and happy for a long time but had hit a rough patch. The weight didn't bother anyone but her.

Merene hoped she would consider doing something besides managing the Glastonbury Market until the end of time. She reminded her mother often that she was smart and beautiful and Novinger was not her final destination. But Dipshit came around on weekends with fistfuls of cash, which was suspect considering he didn't really work.

"Where's the money come from, Mom?" Merene asked. Teresa knew better than to respond.

The last straw came when Dipshit left a few little white pills on the kitchen table, which Merene found when she was getting ready to head to church and eat out afterward at the City with Kenneth and Sharyn.

Too overwhelmed with anger and disgust to confront her mother in person, she left her a note instead. It said, "You can have your boyfriend, but you can't have his bad habits. Otherwise, you can't have your daughter. Choose wisely."

Later that day, Merene stopped back at the house before lunch.

Dalton stood shirtless in the kitchen, scratching himself like an ape. "You need to mind your own business, Cream."

Cream had been Merene's nickname since grade school when an ancient hag of a substitute teacher read the class roster for attendance one morning, trying desperately to decipher the printed names from behind her clunky, cat-eye bifocals.

"Cor—Mer—does that say Cream?" the old woman asked. The class erupted in laughter.

Nicknames, unfortunately, are not often to the liking of the nicknamed. "Cream" stuck, a not-so-veiled reminder that Merene was the only biracial student in Novinger.

Outside of her mother, Kenneth and Sharyn, and Barnabas, the one person who never called her Cream was none other than Jackson Peecher. With a last name like Peecher, the poor boy was doomed to become "Peaches."

Peaches's mother made sure he went to Sunday school every week at Novinger United Methodist Church. Merene's mother made sure she went to Sunday school every week as well.

Mrs. Peecher was a mousy, nervous woman. Her husband was a drunk, the kind who got mean when he'd had too much. And he'd always had too much.

She said she'd leave him for putting hands on her, but she never did. He eventually would lay into his oldest son, welting him up with bruises that he'd have to explain were from flipping over a kayak in the Chariton River or falling from a tree or some other bullshit excuse.

"It's something I have to deal with, I guess," Peaches told Merene as they ate lunch together back in grade school. The pair drew ire and stares from their classmates, who didn't believe that boys and girls should sit together. Cooties were viral and contagious in those days.

Merene was the one person—besides his mother—who knew what Peaches's father did to him. Peaches's dad had served in Vietnam. He got a monthly disability check for being exposed to chemicals and God knew what else over there.

What frustrated Merene most about Peaches was how maddingly calm he was. It might have been due to all of the books he read. A lot of thoughts and ideas floated around in that brain of his. The only people who had read more books than he had were Sharyn and Barnabas, and that was because they had been alive far longer.

"Come back to earth, Peachy."

Merene had to take his books from him sometimes at lunch just to rein him in from his deep thoughts and daydreaming.

"I'm sorry, Merene. I can't really help thinking about thinking."

When he wasn't reading, the tall, lanky kid ran. Miles and miles and miles, his long, skinny legs carrying him over the hills and valleys of Adair County. Merene figured she'd run, too, if her old man were as mean as Peaches's father. The Peechers lived in a house a little outside of town, with a hawthorn tree in front. It was owned by Barnabas. The Peechers had been behind on rent for years.

"Running clears my mind," he told Merene. "Like thinking about you."

If she hadn't loved him before, she loved him then. They were two little old souls stuck in the bodies of children raising themselves the best they could.

The one person Peaches loved as much as Merene was Barnabas Hassan. "Book people always seem to find one another eventually," Peaches told her. "He likes books as much as I do."

He had mowed Barnabas's lawn since he was nine or ten years old. It was the least he could do for their kindly landlord. Not until he was a teenager did Peaches realize his family hadn't paid their grocery tab at the Glastonbury Market for years. It embarrassed him terribly, yet it didn't bother his parents in the least. The only things his parents did pay for were cigarettes and beer and trips to the VA Hospital in Kansas City, when they left their son home alone.

*     *     *

Merene shook her head to bring herself back to the moment with Sharyn and their talk about Merene having left her mother. "I just didn't feel safe around Dipshit anymore. My mom chose him and not me, I guess." Dalton licked his lips like a creepy pervert as he separated Oreo cookies before dunking them into a glass full of Mountain Dew. "Who does that, anyway?"

# CHAPTER SEVEN

Later that same day, after church, Peaches had changed into shorts and a cutoff sleeveless T-shirt. He stopped by the Glastonbury Market on his way to Barnabas's house, where he planned to mow the lawn before heading to Kenneth and Sharyn's for supper.

"Hey, Mother Teresa," Peaches said as he entered.

Teresa sat on a stool with her head leaned back on the wall. She usually greeted people as they walked in, but she remained silent.

He went to a cooler and grabbed a Gatorade. Ranch-flavored peanuts caught his eye as he walked to the counter. He set the items down. Teresa hadn't moved. He crinkled the foil wrapper of the snack to get her attention.

"Mother," he said. "Wake up, Sleeping Beauty. I'm about to shoplift if you don't."

She still didn't move.

Peaches walked behind the counter. The first thing that struck him was that Teresa's lips were unnaturally blue. He placed his hand on her shoulder to try to wake her. He felt for a pulse, remembering the CPR class he had taken as an elective. Like Merene, he was deeply interested in medicine. He knew she was long gone when his fingers felt her neck, cold and clammy.

A few little white pills were clutched in her hand.

"Oh, God."

He closed his eyes, immediately thinking of Merene. Sharyn would have to be the one to break the news to her, Peaches thought. He couldn't do it. Peaches left after he called the county emergency dispatch to report the incident. Barnabas arrived and closed the market for the rest of the day.

"Sharyn's the one to tell Merene," Barnabas said, his voice wavering. It was as if he'd read the young man's mind. "They went out for a drive in the country. They'll be back late in the afternoon."

The thought of Merene's green eyes filling with tears made Peaches's eyes do the same as he started toward Barnabas's place. Accounting for the forty minutes or so it would take Peaches to run, by his estimation, he would have at least an hour by himself to mow before Kenneth, Sharyn, and Merene made it back.

*   *   *

After lunch at the City, Sharyn and Merene made their way to the truck. Merene sat in the middle of the bench seat as they waited for Kenneth.

"How about a drive?" Kenneth said, opening the driver's-side door. "I've been meaning to get out to the La Plata train station. They remodeled it recently. I haven't been there in forever, but I remember the very first time I went there like it was yesterday."

"All right," she said. "I think I'd like to take a drive today."

"Me too," Sharyn said.

They headed south on Highway 63 for the train station in the tiny town of La Plata, which, while freshly renovated, had stood for as long as anybody could remember.

Kenneth began to tell a story. "Did I ever tell you about Willie Seeley?"

"That name sure sounds familiar," Merene said.

"The first time I went to the La Plata station was when Barnabas asked my parents to take in an orphan all the way from New York City. That's been like eighty years ago now. I was probably only six or seven years old."

# CHAPTER EIGHT

---

*Brooklyn, New York City, 1923*

"Smiling eyes are the sign of a pure soul, William."

Sister Mary Catherine worried about the seventeen-year-old more than any other child under her care. He would soon be turned out on his own at eighteen—time for him to be a man. While he could take care of himself, he couldn't navigate the harshness of the world alone.

"Sister," Barnabas Hassan wrote, "I'll see to it the young man is cared for."

It was Sister Mary Catherine who had found him as a baby left on the doorstep of the convent. She spent the night praying that the poor little child would live to see the morning. He had a terrible rattling in his lungs. His tiny body burned with fever.

The fever broke but not without doing its damage. William wouldn't learn to read or write, and he rarely spoke. He grew to be a good boy, listening to the nuns who cared for homeless children before being sent to St. Vincent's Home for Boys once he became a teenager. William held a fondness for babies, especially babies who were very sick. He would often leave his bed for the nursery, where he rocked the littlest ones to sleep, or simply held the babies that cried the loudest. He had a way of soothing them. Sister Mary Catherine was convinced he was a living reminder of what God was: loving, patient, soft, kind.

She never forgot the night when he woke her up to speak one of the few complete sentences he had ever uttered.

"She's in heaven now." William had cradled an ailing baby girl in the final hours of her life, refusing to let her go as he stayed up long past his bedtime. The nuns didn't mind.

Sister Mary Catherine had prayed for a home for young William. He was a good worker and an easy keeper. He was handsome, with dark, wavy hair and smiling Irish eyes. He was skinny as a rail. She marveled at how much the young man could eat.

It was in a time of worried prayer for the soon-to-be-freed man-child that she felt an overwhelming peace and certainty that he should be sent on an orphan train to the Midwest. Surely some kindly farm family could use a hand with their labors. She had heard the farm families in the Midwest always had plenty of food.

"The farmers drink creamy buttermilk with every meal. They grow corn so sweet it might as well be candy," she said to William. William liked the idea of corn as sweet as candy.

She struggled to find words for the handsome young man as she walked him to the train station, holding his hand as if he were a child ten years younger than he was.

"My William." She looked into his cool eyes as she cupped his cheeks with her worn hands. "'May the Lord bless you and keep you. May the Lord make his face shine on you and be gracious to you; may the Lord turn his face toward you and give you peace.'"

"Amen," William said. He was wearing a new suit with new socks and shoes and holding a shiny new rosary in his right hand. A name tag reading "William 'Willie' Seeley, New York City, 1906" was pinned to the right breast pocket of his jacket.

Sister Mary Catherine had packed him food for the train ride to Chicago. A couple dozen children would be making the trip along with him, told nothing more than that they would be heading west to find families to live with permanently. Some were excited by the prospect of the trip on the giant train; others were terrified. William was far and away the oldest in the group. They were all dressed in their Sunday best; their senders knew that making the best impression would help their chances of finding homes.

Sister Mary Catherine had been given a vision of sorts from above. In her dreams, she saw a farmer trudge to a train station to pick Willie up. The farmer and his wife had two younger children, one of whom was a girl. That was the only detail she was clear on.

"The man's eyes are kind, William. You'll know him when you see him."

Willie understood. He was looking forward to having younger brothers and sisters of his own the most, in addition to eating corn as sweet as candy. Maybe he would have a bed. In the orphan home, he slept on a mat on the floor. It got drafty and cold, but he wasn't one to complain.

Willie didn't know how long it took to get to Chicago, but he was excited when they arrived. He would be looking for the man with the kind eyes when he got off the train. He had eaten all Sister Mary Catherine had packed for him.

It was like a family reunion; men and women were united with the picture-perfect children they had dreamed about. The foster families, most hailing from rural areas in the outlying heartland country, had driven to the big city to pick up their orphan train deliveries.

Willie waited on a bench with his name still pinned to his jacket, wearing shoes that were stiff from not being worn.

No one came for him.

The next morning, a smelly old man with greasy hair woke him from the bench he slept on in the train station. Looking him over like a horse buyer, he poked his grimy fingers into Willie's mouth as he checked his teeth. The man shrugged and walked away, uninterested, but then he turned around.

"Boy," he said, "take off your shoes and give them to me."

Willie did as he was told and stood in his socks. Then he went back to sitting on the bench he had slept on. He stayed there through the day until a ticket taker told him he would go back on the train to Missouri. He didn't know what Missouri was, but again, he did as he was told.

He was hungry, and his shoeless feet were cold. His socks had gotten wet.

# CHAPTER NINE

Arthur and Clara Love sat down to eat dinner, the biggest meal served in the middle of the day. It was June and a busy one at that. The father checked in with his wife to make sure their young son had been a good boy while he was out raking freshly cut hay along the Chariton River bottom. He would have to come back to bale it in a day or two after it had dried and cured, smelling sweet as it baked in the warm sunshine.

"He's done everything I've asked, Arthur," Clara said. "He swept the shop, came inside to practice tracing letters on paper, fed the chickens, and gathered and washed their eggs."

"Dad," Kenneth said, "I only got pecked once this time!" He rubbed for emphasis at the red spot on his forearm where the flighty young pullet had attacked. Then he asked, "Can I go with you? I've never been to the train station in La Plata."

"If you're on your best behavior," Arthur said. "For Mr. Hassan."

Kenneth couldn't forget the well-dressed man wearing a suit and a vest with a silk handkerchief in one of the pockets who'd come to visit Arthur Love yesterday evening.

"Mr. Hassan," Arthur said, smiling. "To what do I owe the pleasure of your company?"

It was clear to Kenneth that his daddy had great respect for the well-dressed man. He must be rich or a banker or both, Kenneth thought.

Barnabas was indeed the money man for the Love family. Arthur bought seed and fertilizer and supplies from Glastonbury Market on credit. Hassan, in turn, bought whatever Arthur Love's bottomland farm, Seven Hills Way, produced for the year. Barnabas Hassan paid farmers the market's best prices for the fruits of their growing season's labors. He was as honest as the day was long.

Barnabas had held a stack of books when he came calling the evening before. "I come bearing gifts," he said. "But I'd also like to ask a favor. A young man needs a home, Arthur. He's special."

"For you," Arthur said, "anything."

"We'd love for the young man to stay with us," Clara said. "It's no trouble at all, Barnabas."

# CHAPTER TEN

"I can hear it!" Kenneth said, tugging at his ear, reddened from the bathtime scrubbing his mother had given him. "The motor carriage is coming!"

"Quiet now," Clara said. "Your sister is sleeping."

Arthur smiled, having taken a bath in the big metal washtub himself. He dried off with a hand towel after he finished scrubbing his hands with a clump of homemade soap made from fat and ashes and lye. Store-bought luxuries like milled bar soap were still years into the future for most Chariton River dwellers.

"It's a tin lizzie, Kenneth. A Model T built by Mr. Henry Ford of Detroit, Michigan," Arthur said. "Mr. Ford's workers put it together one piece at a time in a line that never stops moving. It might be the only motor carriage in all of Adair County."

Kenneth watched his mother pack up a basket of food.

"This isn't for you, young man," Clara said. "It's for our guest, who you'll meet at the train station."

Kenneth nodded. The motor carriage was loud. It popped and sputtered and creaked. Clara strained as she picked up her older daughter, Geraldine. She held her with her hands covering the child's ears.

"Stay asleep, baby girl. Stay asleep," Clara said. She kissed her cheek then pointed a finger at her son. "Now you don't get dirty, you hear?"

"Yes, ma'am."

The shirt he wore was stiff with starch, pressed without a single crease.

"Handsome," Arthur said, admiring his son.

"You look nice too!"

Arthur adjusted a brand-new silk tie.

Kenneth took a gasping breath, nearly yelling when he saw Diz, Mr. Hassan's happy-go-lucky terrier dog, bounding out of the moving steel black box a quarter of a mile down their long driveway. The boy was careful and quiet as he opened and shut the front door, but he broke into a full sprint as he raced ahead to meet Diz.

The dog tiptoed as he neared the house, as if he knew Geraldine slept inside. She had fallen gravely ill when she was just a few months old, running an incredibly high fever and enduring intermittent seizures for days. The fever passed, but the meningitis had destroyed the little baby's body. Geraldine would never walk or talk and was prone to seizures when startled by sounds or bright lights. On days when she felt well, she would sit up and smile. She liked to pet Diz.

Arthur and Clara would take turns watching her through the night. They hadn't slept undisturbed for years, but they didn't mind. She was their daughter, and the quiet time was put to good use by the parents for reading and reflecting amid the soft, warm glow of a kerosene lantern as the child dreamed.

Kenneth, by birth order the little brother, became the big brother, and a good one at that. He included Geraldine in everything he did and talked to her like he expected her to reply at any second. The closest she came to words was a stuttered "d-d-d-d."

Arthur liked to think she was trying to say "Dada," but Kenneth knew better. She liked Diz the dog the best. He seemed to understand her need for extra tenderness and care like Kenneth did. Kenneth swore that dog was a human trapped in a furry little suit. He would nod his head as the adults spoke, as if he was a participant in their conversations.

Mr. Hassan had killed the sputtering engine of the Model T not long after Diz bailed. He parked the handsome black vehicle at the end of the long, winding driveway to Seven Hills Way and walked to the house.

"Hello, Mr. Hassan," Kenneth said.

"Hello, young man. You're looking mighty fine this evening. Mighty fine."

The boy stood staring. "You look like a movie star!"

Mr. Hassan wore a three-piece suit with a real silk handkerchief in the breast pocket. A handsome porkpie hat with a flashy red-and-white ribbon, the colors of the Novinger Wildcats, covered his head.

"What do you think?" Mr. Hassan said, looking at the tin lizzie.

"Where do you feed the hay to it to make it run?" Kenneth asked.

"It doesn't eat. It only drinks."

Kenneth couldn't imagine not eating.

Mr. Hassan set down on the front porch a couple of boxes he had carried from the back of the Model T. Arthur and Clara came out to greet their guest.

"Clara, Arthur," Mr. Hassan said, tipping his hat. "I've brought gifts, if that's okay."

"You didn't have to," Clara whispered, still holding Geraldine. "But thank you nonetheless."

"Young man"—he beckoned to Kenneth—"I've got a gift for you." Mr. Hassan handed a perfectly wrapped box to Kenneth. He then handed a larger box to Clara.

"Ladies first," Arthur said.

Clara opened the box to find several yards of fine fabrics from the Baltic Mercantile Company in Europe. There was enough material to make dresses for her and Geraldine, far fancier than the feed-sack dresses she was accustomed to. She brought a hand to her mouth, still holding her sleeping daughter. Tears were in her eyes.

"Thank you," she whispered. Mr. Hassan looked pleased.

Kenneth's eyes were wider than a full moon as he waited patiently for his turn. He opened his box delicately, like an old person. He knew the shredding of gift paper might disturb Geraldine. He uncovered a brand-new pair of broad, squared-toe cowboy boots, monogrammed with KL in exquisite stitching, looking like the brand of a big-time cattle outfit out west.

"I had your initials put on them so your dad wouldn't try to steal them from you."

Diz nudged Kenneth then dug his nose inside of the boots, whose fresh leather scent was manly.

"He wants you to look inside."

Kenneth stuck his hand in the boot, feeling around. In each toe, he found two Cadbury chocolate eggs, all the way from Britain.

"You can have one, son, and save the other for later," Arthur said. "Mr. Hassan already has you spoiled."

Kenneth went over and hugged Barnabas, who wasn't expecting the very sincere physical gesture from the boy.

"Thank you, Mr. Hassan."

He lowered his head in receipt of the thanks. Likewise, Diz lowered his head in the same manner.

The two men started down the dusty drive where the Model T was parked.

"I'm riding in a motor carriage, Geraldine!" Kenneth said in an excited whisper. "I'll tell you all about it when I come home."

Kenneth kissed his sleeping sister goodbye. Diz kissed the little girl as well, brushing his soft, moist doggie nose delicately on her cheek. She smiled, her eyes still closed.

Kenneth sprinted ahead with Diz to catch up to the men. Diz got out ahead of him and then slowed his pace as he neared their ride. The dog let Kenneth win the race there, panting as he looked at the machine as if it were an exhibit in a museum. The boy shared the same sense of awe. Arthur also stood marveling at the contraption.

"You bring it to life with this hand crank under the hood," Barnabas said. "There are three pedals on the driver-side floor: the right pedal is the brake; the middle pedal makes it reverse. The left is the clutch. This here"—he pointed at a hand throttle under the steering wheel—"this here makes it accelerate."

Arthur, with his big, strong farmer's hands, gave the hand crank a spin, summoning the four-cylinder engine to life. It tapped with a steady hum like a snare drum in a jazz ensemble.

"Let's make a deal," Barnabas said. "I'll drive to La Plata, and you drive back. Navigating this steel horse is like dancing with a partner. It requires some patience and finesse."

Too tickled to speak, Arthur clapped his hands. He was eager to try driving the marvel of modern machinery.

Barnabas settled in the driver's seat with Arthur next to him. Kenneth sat on his father's lap. Diz was sandwiched between the two men. In the backseat was a box like the one Kenneth had received earlier. Barnabas had bought their unknown guest a new pair of boots and socks. Clara had received cloth for new shirts and britches for the teenager they would soon fetch. She made her family's clothing by hand, using patterns she ordered from catalogs.

She had only dreamed of fabrics like what had been brought for the family, almost embarrassed to receive such fine products. The gift made Clara wonder who tailored and mended Barnabas's clothes. He was always decked out in high-fashion, gentlemanly attire.

Arthur's hands, each the size of a baseball catcher's mitt, held his young son's cheeks. "She can run forty miles an hour, Kenneth! We'll fly to the train station in no time!"

The leather seats were comfortable as the engine settled into a pleasant clicking rhythm as they headed south. The Model T had a windshield and a topper over their heads but no side or rear windows. The wind was surprisingly chilly as it whipped against the touring sedan in the summer evening.

At the tiny La Plata train station, the conductor became annoyed. A few passengers shuffled out at the stop. A shoeless teenaged boy remained on the train before they turned him out to wait in the station. He looked terrible, scraggly with a few days of stubble, his cheeks hollowed out from missing meals and drinks. His stomach ached with hunger and from worry of the unknown.

Willie Seeley was hunched forward on a bench, rocking back and forth a bit like an old person unsure of their balance. He remembered what Sister Mary Catherine had told him before he left New York City: "The farmers drink creamy buttermilk with every meal. They grow corn so sweet it might as well be candy."

"We're going to be late to Kansas City!" the conductor said.

A visor-wearing clerk sitting in an office booth in the station didn't look up as the complaint was aired. "You won't leave until Barnabas Hassan arrives."

"Who the hell is Barnabas Hassan?"

The clerk shook his head. "Your boss."

Barnabas Hassan had bought the depot and the rail line serving La Plata when the coal mines were really producing. It had proven to be a wise investment, which was unsurprising given Mr. Hassan's "measure twice, cut once" approach to business decisions. He grew tired of the railroad's dishonest practice of giving discounts on shipping to friends and special acquaintances. He figured his coal was as good as anyone's. When the railroad's bonds turned to junk and they went insolvent, he pounced, buying out not only the La Plata depot but everything along the tracks west to Kansas City. He purchased in cash. Cash was king. No one on the railroad lost their jobs in the buyout, which was important to Barnabas. He had a deep and abiding respect for the honest men and women who used their day's wages to nourish and grow their families.

A wiry-looking dog propped his two front legs up on Willie Seeley's knees, apparently looking for an earnest belly scratch. The brush from the small paws startled the young man, who uncovered his face, which he had been holding in his hands. The little dog seemed to be smiling at him. Its bobtail wagged furiously.

The pinhole where Willie's nametag had been placed a week ago was starting to wear, though the letters were still clearly legible.

"He likes you," Kenneth said.

The happiness Willie felt from the surprise visit from the little dog temporarily distracted his mind and stomach from the pangs of hunger.

The deep, resonant baritone of Arthur's voice filled the empty station. "Mr. Seeley."

Diz hopped down from Willie's knee as he stood.

Arthur approached with measured steps. He adjusted his Benjamin Franklin-style spectacles as he prepared to shake the young man's hand. "Kenneth, go get Mr. Seeley his things, please."

Kenneth and Diz scurried off in a rematch of the footrace at the house before they'd left.

Arthur lowered his chin slightly, peeking out over the top of his small lenses, which looked like coverslips for a microscope slide amidst his wide face. He extended his meaty right hand to the teenager. Willie clasped the bear paw before him. Arthur then covered Willie's hand with his left and shook it with genuine warmth.

Arthur's eyes lit up. "Mr. Seeley, we are so glad you came to us. Welcome to Missouri."

Willie heard the echo of Sister Mary Catherine's voice in his head: "The man's eyes are kind, William. You'll know him when you see him."

This man's eyes were kind. This was him.

Sister Mary Catherine was right. She always was.

Barnabas had told Arthur the young man would be shoeless. He was. How could he possibly have known?

Diz raced back to the pair in the train station. Kenneth followed behind, lugging the box and the food that Clara had prepared for their guest.

"Have a seat, young man," Arthur said to Willie.

Willie sat down. The rascal dog Diz grabbed ahold of one of his grimy socks and pulled it off, exposing his bare foot and ankle. He grabbed the other sock and tugged on it.

Arthur opened the box, revealing a pair of brand-new cowboy boots, much like the pair Barnabas had brought for Kenneth. There was a pair of new socks, too, waiting to replace the ones that had served as his shoes since a man walked off with Willie's days ago.

Kenneth was more interested in the food his mother had packed for Willie.

As Willie pulled his new socks on and slid his feet into the new boots that fit like a glove, he caught the smell of biscuits. Kenneth unwrapped one for Willie. They weren't piping hot, but they were still warm in the center.

"This goes with it," Kenneth said. "It's sweet corn chow-chow. You are going to love it!"

The corn spread was bright yellow and smelled equal parts sweet and vinegary. Kenneth carefully separated a biscuit into halves, put a slab of fresh churned butter in the centers, and smeared a generous dab of chow-chow on top. He waited for Willie to take his first bite.

Willie closed his eyes, allowing hunger, the best of the seasonings, a final hurrah. He didn't have to chew the flaky, pillowy biscuit. The butter and flour seemed to melt in his mouth. When he tasted the sweet corn in the chow-chow, he remembered again what Sister Mary Catherine had told him about the farmers and their corn as sweet as candy. She was right. She always was.

Kenneth unscrewed the lid of a mason jar full of thick, frothy buttermilk while Willie ate. He swirled it a bit so that the cream wouldn't separate. He handed it to Willie, and Willie drank the thick liquid. The tartness of the rich buttermilk balanced the sugary sweetness of the chow-chow on the biscuit. If heaven had a taste, Willie thought, it would be something like this.

Kenneth continued to rummage through what his mother had prepared with the enthusiasm a child would have for a friend opening gifts at a birthday party. "You're going to love this too!"

A half loaf of fresh-baked bread emerged. He held a glass dish carefully, looking up at his father to remind him he would be careful not to drop it. Kenneth tore a piece of the bread and scraped some of the chunky contents from the glass dish onto the slice. It was chicken salad, full of meat, creamy mayonnaise, and crunchy bits of celery and green peppers. He reached down farther and found a big, hearty dill pickle wrapped in brown paper. He handed the sandwich and pickle to Willie, who watched him like a dog would watch its master at the dinner table.

Diz wagged his tail enthusiastically the whole time the young man ate.

Barnabas had disappeared once they arrived at the station, presumably to chat with the staff and see if he could find a big-city newspaper from the east. He liked to know what was going on in the world.

The clerk looked up to see the svelte man waiting to speak to him.

"I'd like to send a telegram to New York City."

"Of course, sir."

Barnabas dictated as the clerk typed the message that would soon be relayed to New York City: "Mr. William Seeley arrived safely. Heading to his new home in Novinger, Missouri, in the care of Mr. and Mrs. Arthur Love."

Far away, Sister Mary Catherine closed her eyes after she read the telegram, giving thanks in prayer. She hadn't doubted Willie would make it, but it was nice to have written confirmation of his safe arrival.

"God bless you, Joseph," she said to herself. She knew Barnabas Hassan by the name of Joseph.

Back in La Plata, Kenneth, eager to share his entire world with his new best friend and chattering as young people did, led Willie, comfortable in his handsome new boots, to the Model T. "This is our motor carriage. It's pretty and nice and fast. You're going to love it!"

Barnabas yielded the driver's seat to Arthur, who was almost as giddy as his young son at the prospect of driving the Ford back to Novinger. Kenneth climbed in the backseat with Willie. Diz joined them.

Kenneth yammered on endlessly, explaining every hill and field they passed as they crept north to Seven Hills Way. After half an hour or so, Kenneth realized his new best friend hadn't uttered a word. "You know how to talk, right?"

"Yes," Willie said.

"Okay. Just checkin'."

Arthur looked behind him into the back seat, shouting to overcome the noise of the blowing wind and the hum of the engine. "Kenneth, you haven't taken a breath since we picked up Mr. Seeley!"

# CHAPTER ELEVEN

---

"Kenneth, you haven't taken a breath since we left the City!" Sharyn said.

Kenneth, Sharyn, and Merene had been strolling around the La Plata train station as he recalled the first time he had been there. The train still ran through the town a couple of times a day, headed to Kansas City. The depot had been renovated a few times since Kenneth had gone with his father to pick up Willie Seeley. Kenneth was pretty sure Barnabas Hassan might still own the La Plata depot. If he didn't, it had probably been purchased by the BNSF line when they bought out the old Topeka and Santa Fe railroads.

A plaque in the lobby commemorated the hundreds of children who came to Missouri on the orphan Trains. Kenneth looked at it and froze. "Willie was like an uncle. He never left us until the Lord called him home ten years or so ago."

The three headed back to the truck for the drive to Novinger.

"As long as I live," Kenneth said, pausing for a slow breath, "I'll never forget the first time Willie saw Geraldine." He continued telling his story.

Arthur drove the Model T back to Seven Hills Way, parking it far enough down the driveway so as not to startle his young daughter. Kenneth had fallen asleep in the backseat, resting his head on Willie's lap. Diz had done the same. The trio had become fast friends.

Clara was on the porch, holding her sleeping girl.

"When he saw her, he knew she was special," Kenneth said to the women listening to his tale.

Arthur managed a quiet introduction for Clara and Willie, who was fixated on the sleeping girl. He looked at Clara as he stretched his arms out slightly, asking to hold her. She had sensed he was a gentle soul and obliged.

"Willie held Geraldine all night, rocking her on a chair in the front room," Kenneth said, recalling that first meeting.

Arthur and Clara slept without interruption for the first time since Geraldine had taken sick with the meningitis fever.

"Willie never talked much, only saying a few words at a time. He seemed to understand Geraldine better than anyone. A few years later, when she died, I'll never forget what he said."

"What did Willie say?" Merene asked.

"'She's in heaven now.'"

Merene wiped her eyes with her shirt sleeve. She was silent for a moment until a lightbulb flashed inside her head. She gasped. "Church Over?"

Merene barely remembered the old man who stayed with the nursery attendants and toddlers during services at the Novinger United Methodist Church when she was little. He wore a sharp, fancy suit, his Sunday best. Like clockwork, he would bolt from the nursery in the basement, grabbing handfuls of cookies to pass out to children while proclaiming, "Church over!," earning him the nickname Church Over.

"That was Willie Seeley," Kenneth said.

Merene hadn't realized that before the afternoon ride to La Plata. He had died when Merene was five or six years old. Willie lived with Kenneth after Arthur and Clara Love passed away. He was laid to rest in Kenneth's family cemetery on a bluff overlooking the Chariton River, right next to Geraldine.

As Kenneth's truck inched up the road leading to Seven Hills Way, he looked relieved after sharing his story.

Another light bulb flashed in Merene's mind. "Kenneth," Merene said as she wiped a misty eye, "you can't possibly mean to tell me that Diz has been around since you were a child."

Kenneth raised his eyebrows. He didn't say a word.

# CHAPTER TWELVE

---

"Young 'un, you have time for tea?" Sharyn asked Merene as they walked to the house together. "I've got my own Barnabas Hassan story. I can't get a word in with this old man hangin' around."

Kenneth ventured off to his workshop, where he intended to spend the rest of the afternoon tinkering. Diz had shown up. Barnabas was usually pretty close behind his trusty little dog.

Merene admired Sharyn a great deal. She knew she came from a down-and-out family and had to fend for herself. She had been divorced a long time and lived on her own until she married Kenneth twenty-something years ago. She was a self-made woman. She married Kenneth because she wanted to, not because she had to.

Merene admired the fact that Sharyn could be by herself and still be happy. She spent hours reading alone. She sewed and painted and wrote, though she didn't share what she had written very often.

Years and years ago, Kenneth had gotten into the habit of acquiring donations of clothes, furniture, and tools to give to families who had lost everything in house fires. When Sharyn married Kenneth, they also started a food pantry of sorts at the United Methodist Church. They called the program "PIN," for People in Need.

The people of Novinger saved their plastic grocery sacks and brought them to the Glastonbury Market to be reused. When someone needed food, Sharyn would bag it and deliver it to the market. The family could pick up their order on their own. In this way, they didn't look like beggars and instead appeared no different from any other group of shoppers in Novinger.

From the time Merene was little, she remembered drinking Sharyn's hot teas to help with coughs and colds and tummy aches. Her tea was sweetened with her fresh honey, which tasted better than anything store-bought.  Sharyn kept bees and made her own honey and honey products, including soaps. Kenneth had no interest whatsoever in the hobby. "Men are too impatient to keep bees," Sharyn once told Merene.

Unsolicited, Sharyn spoke up as Merene watched the steam rise from her teacup across the table. "My daddy was a piker from Knox County. He couldn't keep a job."

"What's a piker?"

Sharyn snorted and realized there were two generations separating her and the beautiful young woman sitting across the table. Sharyn didn't think of herself as an old person, but she used antique terms that youngsters weren't familiar with. "A terrible provider, that's what. He was a small-time gambler and a bar fly. My mother was from Hannibal, on the river. I don't know how they met, but it wouldn't surprise me if my daddy was a paying customer of hers."

Merene didn't know what to say and was so shocked that Sharyn noticed she hadn't blinked in an awkward lapse of far too many seconds.

"People are people, Merene. We've got to love 'em all as they are and not as we want them to be. He worked in the coal mines for a while, but as far as I can tell, his gambling debts caught up to him, and he went to drifting again. Barnabas could have thrown my mother and my brother, Virgil, and myself out of his rent house, but you know he's not that kind of man."

"What street did you live on?"

"Gex." In Novinger parlance, the street was pronounced "Jay."

Merene knew the house immediately. It had a perimeter of hawthorns and was one of the few houses that stayed fresh with paint and hadn't fallen into disrepair while it sat empty. As Novinger withered away, many houses had been vandalized and torn apart or set on fire by thrill seekers and miscreants. They stood like scars, a haunting reminder of prosperous times when the mines were in full swing, which was so long ago that no one could remember it or believe Novinger had ever been anything other than tired and withered and decrepit.

It was now a PIN house that the church offered to families who were going through hard times—those that had lost their own homes due to fires or floods or job losses or a string of bad luck. The church didn't ask occupants to pay rent, but they did ask them to maintain the house like it was theirs. It had become a sort of showpiece because of that. Even in his advanced age, Barnabas was a good and able carpenter. He maintained the one-of-a-kind woodwork on that house, keeping it up like something featured on one of those home improvement shows.

"My mother got sick when I was twelve," Sharyn said. "Virgil was ten. If it weren't for Barnabas, I would've dropped out of school. Virgil and I cleaned other people's houses back when people had money in Novinger. We split wood, we delivered coal, did anything to make a buck."

"Where was your dad?"

"I don't know that my dad came around until Mother died. But you don't miss what you don't see. I consider Barnabas Hassan to be my father. He was the one that looked out for us."

"What did she die from?"

"I don't know, but I would guess it was something with her liver. Her skin was as yellow as that"—Sharyn pointed at a pan of cornbread sitting on the table—"before she passed. I was almost sixteen, and Virgil was almost fourteen. By that time, he was as big as a grown man and could pretty much fend for himself. Daddy didn't bother to show up to Mother's funeral. She died in the summer when school was out. Virgil had gone to work a construction job in Saint Louis. I was home alone for a few weeks, though Barnabas and the people of the church checked in on me.

"Daddy came back one night all liquored up, wrecked out of his mind. He pushed me up against a door and kissed me. Not like a father should kiss a daughter."

Merene looked down. She was hoping this story wouldn't turn out the way she feared it would.

"I slapped him hard in the face, and he left me alone. I locked my bedroom door and prayed all night. Time plays tricks on you when you're scared, but sometime during the night, Barnabas came. I knew it was him because I heard Diz barking at my daddy, who had passed out on the kitchen floor."

"Diz can't be that old!" Merene said.

Sharyn smiled and didn't respond. Then she continued after a few sips of hot tea with honey. "I never saw my father again, and I've never missed him. The man who was there for me, Barnabas Hassan, stepped in for good. I wanted to drop out of school, but Barnabas wouldn't let me. I graduated with Diz, Barnabas, and Virgil there to see me walk across the stage—the first in my family. Barnabas threw a graduation party for me that I think, literally, half of Novinger attended. Free ice cream for everyone. That was a good time."

She sipped more of her tea and stared at the floor. "The stress of losing my mother and of my father walking out took a toll on me. I turned on myself to cope. Before I knew it, I put on lots of weight. It's terrible, and it ain't right, but people treat a person so different when they're heavier. Especially women. It's all right for a man to be big and tall and strong. Virgil was thataway. But not for a woman. Imagine that—a double standard! Almost overnight, I got used to being called a heifer, a cow, and worse. What hurt most was that I started to think less of myself because of it."

Merene knew that truth all too well. She wasn't a petite girl by any means. Plenty of people had cruelly reminded her of that fact over the years.

Sharyn went on. "I met Donnie the summer I graduated from high school. I was eighteen, and he was thirty-five. He told me I was pretty and that he loved me. I believed him, even though I knew better. He was no different than my daddy—a smooth talker, a gambler, a skirt chaser. He got me drunk one evening. I passed out but woke up with him on top of me. I was too scared to do anything but wait. I thought if I said anything, he'd leave me. I had myself convinced he was the only man that would ever love me."

Sharyn, typically stone-faced and stoic, trembled. "When I found out I was pregnant, it was Barnabas I told first, not Donnie. I knew

Donnie would be upset. He had already moved on to other lady friends. Barnabas lovingly held me by the shoulders.

"'Sharyn,'" Barnabas said. "'You're the most wonderful person, and you'll be the most wonderful mother.'

"He hugged me so tight I never wanted to let go," Sharyn said. "He wasn't in any way disappointed in me, even though I was disappointed in myself. I begged Donnie to marry me so that my son wouldn't be born out of wedlock, which, in those days, was a powerful way to shame people."

"How stupid can people be to punish a child born into circumstances they can't control?" Merene asked.

"Real stupid."

Merene gave Sharyn a hug. She had known the woman her entire life, but only in the past several minutes had she really gotten to know her.

"After Roger B. was born, Donnie got scared and left."

"Is the B for Barnabas?" Merene asked. She hadn't put two and two together until that moment.

"Roger Barnabas. Named after the man who stood by his mother through thick and thin."

Merene had not remembered anyone calling Roger by only his first name. It was always followed by the B.

"Roger B. grew up big and strong and just barely eked his way through high school. He never liked books."

Roger B. was a welder and raised a few dozen head of beef cattle on hilly pastures west of Novinger. He'd married and had a son and daughter several years older than Merene. He had become what his biological father was not: a respectable man who took care of his family.

"Did you ever worry about being alone the rest of your life?"

Sharyn looked out the window. "I think the best advice Barnabas ever gave me was to let each day take care of itself and not worry about tomorrow. Worry is manmade. And men are the cause of a lot of worry for women in this world!"

Sharyn looked out the window again to see Kenneth fussing and cussing as he banged a hammer on the hay baler, which was notorious for breaking down right when it was most needed.

"When you go to medical school someday"—Sharyn paused as she saw Merene blush—"I want you to explain to me why the men in our species have such thick skulls and such thin patience!"

They both laughed.

"How'd you end up with Kenneth?"

Sharyn looked at the pan of cornbread on the table. "That right there."

"Cornbread?"

"Beans too," Sharyn said. "Kenneth married his high school sweetheart, JoEllen. I knew JoEllen for years and years. She was a lovely woman. She took real sick with kidney failure from diabetes she didn't look after. By the time she went to see a doctor, which she had put off for too long, it was too late. Kenneth took her passing hard. They had been married forty-some years and raised two girls together."

Merene realized she didn't really know Kenneth's daughters. They seemed to have flown the coop and flocked to the big city just as soon as they could.

"Barnabas asked me to bring Kenneth a pot of beans and cornbread one evening. Kenneth, hard to imagine, was skinny as a rail then. He lost a lot of weight after his wife died, doing nothing but farming nonstop to keep his mind off JoEllen."

It was a startling revelation for Merene, like if someone told you Santa Claus had six-pack abs once upon a time. She always knew Kenneth to be big and rotund and happy-go-lucky. She found it hard to imagine him any different.

"We talked until well past dark. He ate more that evening than he had the entire week before. We found that we had a lot in common but were different enough people to find each other amusing. He walked me to the door after we ate to see me out." Sharyn busted out laughing.

"What happened?"

Sharyn tried to restart her recollection but started laughing again. She took her glasses off to wipe the tears from her eyes. She took a deep breath and continued. "He walked me to the door after we ate and tooted on the doorstep as he said goodnight!"

Sharyn set off in a cackling fit, which Merene found more

entertaining than the romantic remembrance of breaking wind years ago. Sharyn got up and went to the bathroom, coming back to pour another tea for herself and Merene.

"Like a gentleman, he asked Barnabas for his blessing to marry me. It had troubled Kenneth terribly that I had been divorced. But Barnabas told him, 'Kenneth, you'd be a fool not to marry her. You know the kind of person she is. That's what matters the most, not what happened in the past.'"

It had been an affirmation of what Kenneth knew to be true deep in his heart.

"Sometimes we need to hear someone else say what we're thinking out loud to reassure ourselves," Sharyn said. "We married when the hawthorns were flowering. Diz was our ring bearer. Only Barnabas was with us."

"Did you have beans and cornbread to celebrate?"

Sharyn looked out the window to see Kenneth joined by Diz, Barnabas, and Peaches, who, by the looks of it, had been crying for a long time. "Stay here for a minute. I'll find out what those men are up to," she said.

Merene stayed at the table, warming her hands on the mug as she sipped the remainder of her tea.

When Sharyn returned, she drew a long breath and took a seat.

"Sharyn?" Merene asked. "What's wrong?"

# CHAPTER THIRTEEN

When she first heard the news of her mother's death from Sharyn, Merene felt relieved. Relieved that she wouldn't have to make Teresa get out of bed and to work on time anymore. Relieved that she wouldn't have to beg and plead and yell at her to take her medication, or attend her addiction support meetings, where people reminded her of the truth: that she was beautiful, smart, and kind. That her best days were ahead of her and not already things of the past.

The teenaged daughter wouldn't have to be the mother anymore. Teresa's sadness and desperation and feelings of insecurity were gone for good.

Next, Merene felt guilty. Guilty that she was relieved her mother had died. Although it defied logic, she felt guilty that her mother had not gone to medical school, as if it were her fault, which she, of course, knew it was not.

When she found out it was the little white pills that killed Teresa, Merene felt rage. Seething, vindictive, fire-breathing rage. Dalton the Dipshit had shared that poison, preying on Teresa's loneliness and insecurity and weakness. Merene figured he was the real killer, not her mother, who had probably mistakenly taken one pill too many.

Last came sadness and a mother-shaped hole in her heart. The hole would shrink with time as the pain eased.

Days later, Sharyn, Kenneth, Barnabas, Peaches, and Merene sat around a table together, planning Teresa Cory's celebration-of-life service, to be held on a Saturday.

Looking at Sharyn, Barnabas spoke. "Before too long, we'll be calling you 'young 'uns' Dr. Peaches and Dr. Merene."

Peaches bowed his head and blushed, accepting the compliment. He wanted to pursue a career in medicine, like Merene. He read every book he could get his hands on and had finished another emergency medicine course in record time, paid for through the volunteer fire department.

By all accounts, the late June afternoon would feature perfectly sunny weather, pleasantly in the mid-seventies for the service. Teresa loved the flowering hawthorns of Novinger. Merene secretly hoped that they would bloom in her honor.

Instead of a somber, traditional funeral service, Merene had decided the best way to remember her mother would be to have an old-fashioned pie supper and auction, with the proceeds going to support drug and alcohol addiction rehabilitation. There would be a dance and a carnival and free ice cream for everyone.

"Funerals are depressing, and depression killed my mother," Merene said. "The best way to celebrate her is for everyone to be happy and have a good time together. She would have liked that."

Barnabas Hassan paid for everything. It was the least he could do for her and for Teresa, he told Merene. They were the finest employees in the history of the Glastonbury Market.

Kenneth, Peaches, and Barnabas had been busy planting hawthorns throughout the city in remembrance of Teresa Cory. Diz helped by pawing out dirt and diving down holes that eventually swallowed the little dog from sight. Merene had lost count, but there had to have been hundreds of new trees planted in the week leading up to the celebration of life and the pie-supper festivities that would follow. She closed her eyes, thinking of her mother's face. They would soon be blooming for her, she thought.

The celebration-of-life service for Teresa Cory was simple and heartfelt. The church was packed, and songs to suit several musical tastes were played. Teresa was a huge fan of the Allman Brothers, much to the chagrin of Kenneth. He wasn't a fan of anything but twangy country. Anything outside of that was deemed "long-hair music."

They played her favorite Allman Brothers song, which happened to be entirely instrumental. It was lively, the kind of song that made a person feel happy and free and want to jump to their feet and give dancing a try even if they couldn't dance. As the electric piano echoed with the tune, Merene closed her eyes again. She saw her mother's face, and she was smiling. And dancing.

She opened them for a minute to see Barnabas, eyes closed, nodding his head and tapping his toe to the music as he sat in the church. Diz was keeping tune, wagging his tail in rhythm. Barnabas really liked the Allman Brothers. It was a bond he had shared with Teresa.

A gentle breeze moved through the open windows of the church on that Saturday. After the song finished, Merene stood with Peaches. He took her hand as they walked down the aisle of the church past the rows of pews, which were full. Kenneth and Sharyn followed behind, trailed by Barnabas and Diz.

When they made it to the back of the church, Peaches slipped Merene a quick kiss. He smirked and opened the church doors to the outside.

There had to have been a thousand people lining the street. The volunteer fire department, wearing starched and pressed uniforms with hair well-oiled and slicked down into place, stood at attention. Clapping, clapping, clapping was all Merene could hear as Peaches held her hand as they walked. When they made it to the school, a huge banner with a picture of Teresa's face was hanging from an outdoor stage and dance floor. A legion of grills sizzled. Barnabas had arranged to serve the crowds fish and hamburgers and hot dogs and ice cream.

Merene walked past a collection of tables where pies sat waiting to be auctioned. "There has to be hundreds of them!" she said to Peaches. "Look at that pretty mincemeat pie with the lattice top. Mom would like that one."

"So would Barnabas," Peaches said.

"Kenneth ruined mincemeat for me when I was in grade school.

He told me that minces were tiny little furry creatures the size of mice that you diced up to make the pie. I'm not about to tempt fate to find out if he was joking or not."

The pie supper would begin at seven p.m., with music and dancing to follow. Until then, Barnabas had booked a carnival for people to enjoy at no cost. There were ponies to ride; a Ferris wheel; a big, tall slide that you went down on a burlap sack; and a dozen carnival games. There were balloon animal makers and face painters and bounce houses. This was the closest thing to Walt Disney World kids in Novinger would ever experience.

The celebration was the biggest party Novinger, Missouri, had seen in a long time. Teresa Cory would have been proud of her little town. And Merene was treated like a queen. She had hugged about a thousand people by the time of the pie auction.

"I'm not going to sit around and be waited on," she told Peaches. "Let's get to work."

She served food alongside Peaches and Sharyn. People might have come to the celebration saddened by the loss of Teresa or the loss of one of their own family members to addiction, but their blues soon dissipated like a bright, warm sun was burning through a hazy fog.

Peaches looked over at Merene from time to time just to stare. He was so proud she was his. And Merene was proud the scrawny boy she had known forever had grown up to be such a kind person.

A microphone popped and cracked. The crowd clapped and whistled.

"Teresa, we love you," Kenneth said. "Our first pie in the sale is mincemeat, Teresa Cory's favorite. Can I get one thousand dollars?"

A volunteer firefighter walked back and forth across the stage, showing off the pie. It looked like a work of art.

"Five thousand dollars!" someone yelled.

"Five, now, six, now, can I get a…" Kenneth hummed as he rattled away in an auctioneer's cadence.

Merene lost track of the bids until she heard twenty thousand. The bidding stalled there then made a steady climb upward.

"Forty-nine, now, now, now, can I get a fifty, now, now, now, can I get a fifty?" Kenneth sang. "Fifty thousand dollars!"

The audience broke out in applause.

"Fifty, now, now, now can I get a..."

Barnabas hadn't changed from the sharp dress clothes he'd worn to the church earlier in the day. He'd donned a three-piece suit and porkpie hat. He looked like a character from a Charles Dickens novel.

The bidding was cooling off.

Barnabas was sitting. He put his hands to his knees, rocking forward gently to get the momentum to stand upright. He was elderly, after all, though he looked and acted like a much younger man. He grabbed his hat and tipped it down. He pointed at Kenneth, who raised his chin and curled his lip, as if he were about to catch a piece of food in his mouth.

Barnabas raised his right index finger in the air, making a "one." Kenneth nodded.

He made a circle with his thumb and index finger. Kenneth nodded.

Barnabas did it again.

"Attention, Novinger, Missouri. Barnabas Hassan likes mincemeat pie. We have one hundred thousand dollars!"

The crowd roared and jumped to their feet.

"Sold to Barnabas Hassan!"

A woman who represented Adair County's drug and alcohol addiction recovery center waved on the stage and bowed in thanks for the incredible donation.

Except for the fact that Merene's mother wasn't there to celebrate, the day couldn't have been more perfect.

# CHAPTER FOURTEEN

———

"Lord," Kenneth said, "now I know how you must have felt feeding the five thousand!"

Lines of hundreds of people waited for Barnabas's ice cream. When the music and dancing started as dusk came, the people seemed to multiply.

Kenneth wheeled an empty ice cream barrel to a tent out of view from the crowds. "Go dance for a minute," Kenneth said to Peaches. "But first, find Barnabas for me and send him my way."

"I can't dance to save my life," Peaches said.

"If it makes you feel better, neither can I. Go get Barnabas. I need him right quick."

Peaches darted out into the crowd. He found Barnabas and sent him to Kenneth.

Barnabas removed his hat when he was under the cover of the tent, alone with Kenneth. Diz stood watch nearby.

"We're out of ice cream, boss man," Kenneth said. "And the night is still young."

Barnabas smoothed his hair with the palm of his hand. Diz came inside the tent, carrying a wooden staff in his mouth.

"Put the lid on that barrel," Barnabas said. "Look away for a moment."

Kenneth did as he was told. He heard Barnabas tap the empty ice cream barrel with Diz's big stick.

Kenneth stared at his feet until there came a light so bright he was temporarily blinded, like with the instantaneous flash from a Polaroid camera. The brightness subsided as quickly as it came. Kenneth could see again.

"Try some," Barnabas said. The previously empty ice cream barrel was filled to the brim.

Kenneth poked a finger into the sweet, cold creaminess. "You saved the best for last," Kenneth said. "It's delicious. Can I get some wine while you're at it?"

"Thanks be to God," Barnabas said. "Don't press your luck." He put his hat back on and left the tent.

Kenneth wheeled the heavy ice cream barrel to Sharyn, who waited with gloved hands to serve scoops to a queue of people that continued to grow.

"I told you he wouldn't let it run out," Sharyn said to Kenneth.

As Sharyn doled out portions, the barrel never emptied. No one knew. No one except Kenneth and Sharyn and Barnabas Hassan.

Diz knew, too, but dogs were good at keeping secrets.

Not too far from the tent, Merene embraced Peaches during a slow dance. She rested her head on his shoulder, comforted by the unshakable beating of his heart.

When the song finished, he hugged her. "I've got a long run tomorrow. I've got to get to bed." He kissed her on the cheek and headed home.

She would be moving into the house next to Kenneth and Sharyn's on Seven Hills Way for the next year until she graduated, something she was looking forward to.

Merene said goodbye to several people as she decided to head out not long after Peaches. Walking away from the dance floor, she heard a familiar voice.

"Can I get a kiss?" Dalton asked.

Merene didn't turn around to acknowledge him. She kept on, heading to a grassy pasture where her car was parked.

"Can I get a hug?" Dalton asked.

She shook her head, walking faster.

"Please? I want a squeeze. See if you're as good as your momma."

Merene sprinted across the field. Dalton took off after her. She got to her car with shaky hands. No one was within earshot of them.

Dalton licked his lips like a pervert. "I dream about you, Cream. Naughty dreams."

Merene couldn't look him in the face. She didn't want to give him the satisfaction of seeing her cry. She glanced down and saw that Diz was hiding under the driver's-side door of her car.

Then Barnabas emerged from out of nowhere. "Sir, you need to leave," he said.

"Shut the hell up, old man."

Barnabas looked down. "I don't suppose you heard me, young man. You need to leave. Right now."

"Or what?" Dalton said, almost spitting. Agitated, he twitched and jerked and scratched the side of his neck compulsively. He took a few steps toward Barnabas with a balled, white-knuckled fist.

Barnabas chuckled and stood his ground. Diz yipped and growled as he came out from under the car.

"Sir, this is the last time I'm going to ask you to leave."

The repeated pleasantry seemed to anger Dalton the most.

Merene was looking at Barnabas, frozen. She didn't know what she would do if Dalton attacked him. She hoped Diz would make enough noise to draw someone's attention from the celebration in the distance.

Barnabas removed his hat with his left hand. He leaned his face forward, bringing his right hand, cupped, under his chin. He blew a kiss to Dalton.

It was a calm and still night. Out of nowhere, a straight-line, gale-force wind stirred.

The gust knocked Dalton from his feet, flat onto his back like he had caught a devastating uppercut from the heavyweight boxing champion of the world. The wind emptied Dalton's pockets. Out came a baggie filled with white dust, which glimmered in the twilight. Another baggie held enough little white pills to fill an aspirin bottle.

While Dalton was on his back, a man approached him, surveying the scene. The man took a look at Dalton on the ground and shook his head. He flashed him his badge.

"It ain't mine!" Dalton hollered. "It's that old man's!"

Apparently, he had forgotten about Merene, who was somewhat hidden behind her car door.

Diz was shaking his head. He approached Dalton cautiously and lifted his leg. He sprayed a few squirts in his face.

"Oh, you little bastard!"

The sheriff's deputy began reciting lines from memory. "You have the right to remain silent. Anything you say can and will be used against you in a court of law. You have the right to speak to an attorney and to have an attorney present during questioning."

Diz started barking as the sheriff's deputy cuffed Dalton and lifted him to his feet.

As they walked off, Merene gathered her composure. "Hey, Dalton," she said.

He turned around and glared. She blew him a kiss.

There were no gale-force winds to accompany it.

Amidst the fray, she hadn't noticed Barnabas slip off into the night. She felt like she had to find him to thank him for sticking up for her. After she fixed her makeup and hair, using the mirror in her car, she went back to the celebration and helped serve ice cream until midnight, when they finally closed everything down.

Barnabas and Diz walked her back to her car. She gave him a hug. "Thank you."

Diz barked excitedly, wagging his tail.

She drove toward her new home next to Kenneth and Sharyn, which they had given to her rent-free. It had been an emotionally exhausting day, filled with highs and lows, fear, excitement, and love. As her car meandered through town out into the country, she noticed something that she hadn't earlier in the day. All the hawthorns had flowered.

"There's no way." In that moment, she thought that Barnabas Hassan commanded both the wind and hawthorn blooms. But that was ridiculous. She laughed.

When she got out of her car to head to the little house next to Kenneth and Sharyn's, she swore she heard the piano riffs from the Allman Brothers song echoing in the wind. Merene looked up at the stars. "I love you, Momma."

# CHAPTER FIFTEEN

———

"It's not my dope," Dalton Reese said to the sheriff's deputy. They sat in a brightly lit interview room at the county jail after he'd spent the night locked up.

"I didn't say it was yours, Reese. I want to know where you got it. If you don't do some explaining, you're going to be adding manslaughter to your possession charges. These pills are the same ones that killed Teresa Cory."

An attorney the county provided to the accused whispered in Dalton's ear. "This is serious. You had better tell them everything, you know."

Dalton cleared his throat. He swallowed. "A friend of mine arranged for me to meet this guy in a barn out in the middle of nowhere a few days ago. It was almost dark."

"Why did he want to meet you?"

"This guy knew I was with Teresa Cory. He asked my friend about her specifically, said he knew she worked for that rich old man."

"Barnabas Hassan?"

"Yeah."

"Go on."

"The guy was sitting at the end of a table in a barn. I couldn't see his face. He was wearing sunglasses. Pale as hell. Almost pure white. I went to the end of the table and grabbed the stuff that was there for me.

When I did, I almost threw up. He smelled so bad. You know what a meth lab smells like? Worse than that. Like something was spoiled and rotten. This dude just sat there like nothing bothered him at all."

"Did he say anything?" the deputy asked.

"I took the stuff at the end of the table. I turn to walk off, and I see the guy is playing with something in his hands. I try to be friendly, even though I'm trying not to gag. 'What's your name, man?' I asked. Then I see he's got a black snake in his hands. A real, live snake. He lets it slither up his arm to his neck until it's wrapped around it like a scarf or something."

The deputy closed his eyes and brought his hand to his forehead. "Let me get this straight, Reese. A stinking, pale man wearing sunglasses, sitting alone at a table in the middle of a barn, is fondling his pet snake. In the dark. You watch too many movies, son. That's ridiculous."

"I'm not lying."

"Then what was his name?"

Dalton took a deep breath and swallowed. "Jest-ess," he said. "Or something like that."

The deputy saw the prickle of goose bumps appear on Dalton's arms. "What kind of name is that?"

"Hell if I know. It's not a name you forget."

"Anything else, Reese?"

"His voice was freaky. The dude groaned when he spoke, like he was pissed off or in pain. I got the hell out of there and never saw him again."

# CHAPTER SIXTEEN

———

After church on Sunday, Merene skipped the weekly pilgrimage to the City with Kenneth and Sharyn. She packed a picnic lunch for herself and Peaches. They had an important, though somber, visit to make. Merene wouldn't let Peaches make the trip alone. She loved him too much not be there with him.

It was the one-year anniversary of the death of Brady, Peaches's kid brother and only sibling. Peaches was eight years old when Brady was born. Carrying his brother home from the hospital in Kirksville was one of the best days of his life. The two boys forged an immediate, lasting bond. In short order, Peaches became not only an older brother but a parent. His parents' alcoholism left a void in their children's lives. Peaches made sure Brady would never go without because of it.

By the time Brady started school, it was Peaches who got him up and dressed in the morning, packed his lunch, and made sure he got off to school on time. It was Peaches who planned his brother's birthday parties, arranged money from the Tooth Fairy, and made sure Santa knew what Brady wanted.

"When I grow up," Brady wrote for a school assignment, "I want to be like my brother, Peaches." He drew a picture of a peach and a stick figure running fast across a race finish line. The next line read "Peaches is #1!" in the chunky, sloppy handwriting characteristic of elementary school years.

One day Brady said, "I can't see, Peaches. It's blurry."

Peaches thought little of the complaints when they first surfaced. Brady probably just needed glasses. Then came the headaches, which, over the course of a few short weeks, escalated in severity. Peaches took off school to take Brady to the doctor in Kirksville. Merene joined them. Sharyn drove. His mother and father stayed at home. They were in no shape to drive by late afternoons, both of them joking about and relishing their habit of beer and cigarettes for breakfast and lunch. Neither of them ate much of anything anymore. Their diets were almost entirely liquid.

The first doctor's visit was uneventful. They checked Brady out and did a battery of routine tests. A lingering sinus infection might be to blame. He had been coughing and sniffling. As a precaution, the doctor, with a medical student in tow, recommended an MRI to take a look at Brady's brain and spine. Peaches and Merene were mesmerized by the doctors at the hospital. Medicine was such an exciting field and a way to make a real difference in the world.

"We're going to take a picture of what's inside that noggin of yours," the kindly doctor explained to Brady. "We know it's full of brains!"

Brady was exceptionally intelligent and perceptive, due mostly to his desire to keep up with Peaches. Since Brady was more or less Peaches's child, he didn't raise him on baby talk or simplistic explanations. He spoke to him like an adult, explained the world to him like an adult, and expected him to carry himself with the poise and self-control of someone much older. Brady was an "old soul" like his brother.

Nightly reading to Brady made Peaches a better student. Eager to keep up with his big brother, Brady refused to read "baby" books in second grade, instead preferring to hear about what his brother was learning.

"Biology," Peaches told his brother, "is the study of life. All living things are made up of tiny little pieces called cells."

"It forces me to understand things better when I have to break it down and explain in ways that he can understand," Peaches told Merene. "I learn and then teach what I've learned to him."

Brady was fascinated when Peaches described the tables and exhibits and pictures in his high school textbooks in incredible detail.

At the hospital, Peaches made a game of describing what the MRI would be like. "You're going to be in a space shuttle," Peaches said. "And I'll be watching you from behind a window." Brady would have to stay very still as he went into a giant tube that took magnetic images of the inner workings of his skull.

One morning Brady said, "Turn the lights on, Peaches! Quit messing around. I need to get to school!"

Peaches was making Brady breakfast before school, and they were expecting to receive the MRI results that week. A few moments before, he had flipped on his kid brother's bedroom light and laid out his outfit on the bed after reminding him to brush his stinky teeth.

"Peaches!" Brady yelled. "Turn the lights on! It's dark in here!"

Peaches was finishing up frying a couple of eggs with a slice of cheese melted on top. He grabbed an English muffin from the toaster so he could assemble a breakfast sandwich. At his brother's shouts, he went upstairs. Brady was stalling. He must've stayed up past his bedtime playing video games, typical eight-year-old behavior.

"Buddy," Peaches said. "Let's get ready to go."

"It's dark. I can't see a thing!" Brady cried. "I can't see."

Peaches walked over to Brady, who was sitting up in his bed. He held out a paper plate with the breakfast sandwich for him.

Brady's eyes looked glassy. Peaches watched Brady use his hand to probe the plate and find the food by touch. He wasn't joking about being in the dark. He couldn't see a thing.

"Eat your breakfast, and I'll let you sleep in a bit. You must've stayed up too late. You're a video game addict!" Peaches forced himself to laugh to reassure his kid brother that the episode was no big deal. Despite his cool demeanor, Peaches was scared out of his mind.

Barnabas came with Merene as the doctor and medical student made a house call to break the news to the family. After an exploratory biopsy, they would later find out that a rapidly growing, aggressive brain tumor was putting pressure on Brady's optic nerve, causing temporary bouts of blindness along with crippling, persistent headaches.

That was a Friday evening near dinner time. Peaches's dad went to his shop to drink while his mother put a movie on for Brady to watch.

Peaches, overwhelmed by the news, did the only thing that eased his mind. He ran as far as he could.

Hours later, Merene picked up the ringing phone at work and answered. "Glastonbury Market. This is Merene speaking."

An old woman's voice crackled. It was long past her bedtime. "A young man out running asked me to call you to pick him up. Poor thing is tired and thirsty. Says he would like three Gatorades and a Snickers."

It was almost midnight, close enough to the market's normal closing time. "Yes, ma'am. Can you give me your address?"

The trip from Novinger west to the woman's house was over thirty miles—Merene watched the trip meter roll over as she arrived. Peaches was sitting on a patch of grass in front of a tidy-looking old farmhouse set back from the winding trail of Missouri Highway 6 west of Milan.

When Merene got Peaches in the car, helping him with her arm over his shoulder as he hobbled like a wounded soldier, he started bawling. His feet were bleeding, but the physical pain paled in comparison to the pain of knowing Brady wasn't long for this world. They sat in the car at the end of the driveway of some country lane in the middle of nowhere for an hour before Merene started the car for home.

# CHAPTER SEVENTEEN

Brady's cancerous affliction was aggressive and rare. Peaches shaved his head in solidarity with his brother, whose hair fell out after his first wave of an experimental radiation treatment. Doctors advised, as a precaution, that the family keep several feet away from Brady for the days immediately after he received treatment. Peaches ignored the warnings and let Brady sleep with him, keeping watch at night as his little brother heaved and huffed and vomited. He waited until Brady was asleep to cry.

When the experimental treatments were found to be ineffective, it was determined that Brady would be kept as comfortable as possible.

Merene got into the habit of stopping by Peaches's house in the mornings to check in on the boys. She mostly wanted to make sure Peaches was eating. He went on self-imposed hunger strikes when Brady got to the point of being unable to stomach food and the doctors outfitted him with a feeding tube.

There were sparkles of hope and laughter when Barnabas came for visits. Brady always seemed to be able to keep down the ice cream Barnabas brought for him, and he enjoyed the fact that Diz ate ice cream with them out of a "pup cup."

Peaches tried to fill Brady's good days with as much fun as he could handle, though his fragile body tired easily. They went fishing together at the Thousand Hills State Park and rented a paddleboat, which was paid for by Barnabas. He also surprised the boys with a weekend trip to Kansas City, where Brady visited the Worlds of Fun amusement park. They stayed in a fancy downtown hotel. Sparing no expense, Barnabas rented a limousine and driver.

Peaches's mother and father were as supportive as the alcohol they depended on allowed them to be. No parent should live to see the death of their child. Peaches's father took the situation the hardest, locking himself in his shop to smoke and drink and cry alone, unbothered. This had driven a wedge between the father and his oldest son, who wanted to cry more than anyone but had to be strong for Brady. Peaches found brief respite from grief during his long runs, when his body became so exhausted that his mind relented and was too tired to be sad.

"I wish I knew why bad things happen to the innocent," Barnabas told Peaches. "It's a question that has plagued mankind for a long time."

Barnabas had introduced Peaches to, in his own words, "his friend Ignatius." Ignatius Loyola, a soldier who founded a religious society committed to teaching and working to help others, had written about spiritual awakenings some four hundred fifty years ago. Peaches found comfort in Loyola's writings.

He decided while out on a long run that once Brady had passed away, he would join the military sooner rather than later. If nothing else, it would get him far, far away from Novinger, which would be welcome, except that it meant he would be separated from Merene.

The night before Brady went to sleep for the last time, he spoke to his brother next to him. "You think you can keep secrets from me because you're older," Brady said. Smiling, the bald-headed, jaundiced boy laughed. "But you can't. Barnabas and Dismas told me all about how beautiful heaven will be."

Peaches cried.

"You love Merene," Brady said. "I know because you kiss her. Kissing girls is gross. She loves you, and you two will get married. And someday, there will be a little Brady." He giggled. "My nephew. In case you didn't know, that means you will kiss Merene and have a baby together."

Sensing the pain in his older brother's shaking body, Brady wrapped Peaches up in the strongest hug his weakened body could muster. The brothers fell asleep intertwined, holding one another with arms folded like pretzels.

It was Merene who found the two brothers sleeping in that same embrace in Peaches's bedroom the next morning. And it was Merene's turn to hold Peaches when he awoke and Brady did not.

Now she stood at the Seven Hills Way cemetery with Peaches. They couldn't believe Brady had been gone a year already. They would be seniors that fall, graduating and starting new lives.

Peaches asked Barnabas what he thought about his plan to join the army, which would send him to basic training not long after the state cross-country championship in a few months. Peaches was expected to be a qualifier and a serious contender at the state meet.

Barnabas, kind and wise, didn't steer him one way or another. "I trust your judgment, young man."

It was practical.  He would serve in the military and then come home to go to school with Merene. He knew, as she knew, that they would be married someday. Oddly enough, they had never verbalized what they both felt so strongly.

Staring at Brady's grave, the grass bumpy and not yet smoothed over by the final settling of the casket below, Peaches spoke up. He held Merene's hand as he sniffled. "I've got to get away for a while."

Peaches told Merene about Ignatius Loyola and how Loyola became a soldier and then decided he didn't want to be a soldier forever. He talked about his feelings and about how he loved her more than anyone. He told her about his last conversation with Brady and how Brady had described their life together.

Merene wiped her eyes and shook her head. "So, you have to find yourself by leaving me here alone?"

"If I thought for one second that I wouldn't come back to you, I wouldn't even think about leaving." He paused for a long while, then he produced a small box. "I suppose a cemetery isn't the most romantic of places to give this to you."

Merene opened the box to find a promise ring with a heart-shaped stone set on a sterling silver band. The vibrant green chrome diopside gemstone almost matched the deep hue of Merene's eyes.

The playful yapping of Diz interrupted the moment, which had been sentimental enough to have been a vignette from a sappy, romantic, made-for-TV movie.

Barnabas moved toward them, taking careful, ginger steps, showing his age. Kenneth and Sharyn weren't far behind him.

"Oh, to be young and in love!" Kenneth said, in jest.

When Merene slipped the ring on her finger, she knew that Sharyn must have advised Peaches on his purchase. It fit perfectly. No way had a teenaged boy paid attention to ring sizes appropriate for women.

Kenneth shook his head, talking to Peaches while he glanced over at Sharyn. "Thanks a lot, young man. Now she's going to expect me to get her a new ring. That sounds expensive."

Barnabas lingered at Brady's grave as everyone else started back home. Merene waited as he paid his respects, closing his eyes and moving his lips. Then he said, "He'll be all right, Merene. I know he'll come home."

"How do you know?"

"I know."

The old man's preternatural confidence settled the young woman's fears, at least for the moment.

# CHAPTER EIGHTEEN

*"The best pace is a suicide pace, and today looks*
*like a good day to die."*
*—Steve Prefontaine*

"Stop it! You've got to stop showing off!" the cross-country coach screamed.

Peaches liked to race as a front-runner from start to finish, a dangerous tactic employed by a world-class distance athlete he adored, Steve Prefontaine. Prefontaine was known to shoot ahead right from the start, never relinquishing a lead. Common sense would dictate that a distance runner keep pace with a pack of competitors for a while before carefully separating in the home stretch to take the lead.

"Good run, Rats," Peaches said to his teammates, after practice ended. "Let's hydrate."

While officially the Novinger Wildcats, the whole town preferred the city's unofficial nickname, the River Rats. No one seemed to be ashamed of the epithet used for years to denigrate the sons and daughters of the miners and farm folk who made their homes along the Chariton River.

"Thank God we weren't born in Unionville," Kenneth said while watching one of Peaches's cross-country meets. "Can you imagine what it must feel like to be a Putnam County Midget?" Putnam County's mascot was, indeed, a midget.

Peaches and the River Rats hadn't had serious challengers all season. They left everyone behind at meets across northeast Missouri, winning in Brashear, in Macon, and at the regional meet in Columbia. The boys sported long rattail haircuts spouting out of the backs of their heads, and the girls' squad followed suit with tightly braided rattails to match. Peaches, their captain, was the lone outlier. He maintained the same razor-shaven dome he had worn the entire time Brady had been sick and lost his hair. He hadn't let his hair grow since his brother died.

Half of Novinger came to cross-country meets to cheer on their hometown. The River Rat fan section wasn't hard to pick out. Younger fans sported rattails or braided hair with red-and-white ribbons woven into the plaits. Young and old alike painted whiskers on their faces, making them look like real-life versions of their unofficial rodent mascot.

Kenneth even let Sharyn paint whiskers on his face for the Columbia meet. When Peaches saw him after crossing the finish line as the overall winner and within striking distance of a state record time, he fell over, writhing on the ground. When he finally caught his breath, his concerned teammates and cheering section were pleased to see him laughing, confirmation that he could still, in fact, breathe and that he hadn't suffered some sort of heart attack or stroke after the impressive athletic feat.

The River Rats' victory song was "Rat Salad," a bass-guitar and drum-heavy instrumental tune by Black Sabbath. It had taken some coaxing and an assurance that the song wasn't a satanic summoning to get the older folks to accept it, but the team and their fans regularly headbanged to it in unison, rattails and whiskers proudly on display.

"Not bad for long-hair music," Kenneth said.

The meet in Columbia had drawn big crowds. A little over a month later, the state championship would be held in Jefferson City.

"I guess I should be jealous," Merene said to Peaches as he sipped water at the finish line, waiting for all of his teammates to cross. "They're checking you out."

The admiring onlookers were hard to miss. Slick-looking young men in matching tear-away pants and brand-new track jackets laughed as they saw hardscrabble country kids cross the finish line in uniforms that looked like they were older than the runners themselves. The academy team had matching shoes in their school colors, a far cry from the ragtag shoes the River Rats raced in. They had come to scope out their competition and didn't appear to be impressed.

"Rich kids," Merene scoffed.

A cluster of boys huddled around their leader, whose jacket read Business on the back. Clayton "Business" Buys was straight out of a fancy private Catholic academy in Saint Louis. He was the only runner in the state who was coming close to Peaches's split times and his dominance at meets. "Business" looked more like a stud baseball player than a distance runner. He was tall and broad-shouldered and tanned. He wore a big gold chain around his neck, accented by unusually large, straight front teeth that shined like a spotlight when he smiled. In contrast, Peaches was lanky and stringy and looked like a strong wind would cut him in half. He leaned forward as he ran and kept his hands held high, like a boxer protecting his chin. Merene found this look peculiarly endearing.

Business walked over to Peaches, who was still focused on the race. "Good run, Rat."

Peaches nodded. They hadn't been introduced to one another but knew they were rivals.

Business then walked right in front of Peaches, blocking his view of the course. "Get used to looking at my ass. It'll be in front of you next month." He slapped Peaches on the back, like they were old friends. He cocked his head to the side to acknowledge his posse, who laughed on cue.

Merene was incensed.

"You're kind of cute," Business said to her.

He put his gold chain in his mouth either to show it off or maybe to chew at it out of nervous habit.

"You're kind of… not," Merene said.

After the last River Rat finished, Peaches straightened. "I wish you the best, man." He moved forward to shake the hand of his rival, only to find that Business had turned his back to give him the cold shoulder.

"Hey," Peaches said.

Business looked at him.

"Nice ass."

# CHAPTER NINETEEN

Novinger traveled en masse to Jefferson City for the state championship meet. The state's capital would host a very hilly and windy course for the cross-country runners to navigate. The last half mile leading to the finish was a slow and steady incline. It would destroy the unconditioned and those who started the race too fast.

Peaches and the River Rats liked their chances, given that their training miles logged along country roads in the peaks and valleys of northeast Missouri leading up to the state meet were equally hilly and windy. Flatlanders wouldn't fare so well on the steep and grueling course.

"You're not running for yourself or your teammates," the coach reminded the team. "You're running for your community. We are proud of every one of you."

Barnabas paid for the runners to travel the night before and stay in a hotel with a complimentary continental breakfast. Unaccustomed to such luxuries, the kids greatly enjoyed their accommodations, taking the small soaps and shampoos from the rooms home as souvenirs. He made the trip alongside Kenneth, Sharyn, Merene, and Diz.

The team walked the course beforehand, carefully talking through pacing and twists and turns. Barnabas traversed the 5,000-meter jaunt as well, listening to the deliberations and planning amongst the athletes and Peaches, their unflappable leader.

The coach admonished his hairless captain. "You can't be front-running the whole race on a course like this. You'll run out of gas. Stay in a pack and separate at the end. If you don't, your slick private-school buddy will eat you alive."

Peaches understood. He would have to watch out for Business, who would be the strongest competition he had seen yet.

Barnabas bought the team new matching Mizuno running shoes in River-Rat red and white a couple of weeks before the state meet so the runners could have ample time to break them in. The flashy kicks were customized, emblazoned with the outline of a river running the length of the shoe. The rear portion of the heel had a rattail. Merene was the artistic inspiration behind the design. After witnessing glowing approval from the runners, she was convinced, like Barnabas, that the shoes were perfect.

Peaches couldn't believe how fast he felt in his pair. They were so incredibly lightweight and perfectly cushioned. The shoes boosted the spirits of the runners, fighting back their impostor syndrome as they would soon line up against far wealthier competition from across the state. They had earned a spot at the state meet. The new shoes helped convince them they belonged and could hang with the best Missouri had to offer.

After his team finished dinner on Friday night, the coach spoke up, with a pained look on his face. Several boxes had been brought into the restaurant. He choked up. "I'm proud of each and every one of you. Ladies and gentlemen, tomorrow morning, we're running not for ourselves but for each and every person in Novinger, Missouri, and—" He paused to take a long, hard swallow. "We're running for Brady."

The coach unpacked new, lightweight compression singlets with matching shorts. They looked as fancy and modern and synthetic as what a world-class Olympian would wear. They were red, with "Novinger" in white lettering on the front. The coach had obtained special permission from the school board to add "For Brady" on the back of every uniform. To top it off, each runner received a new track jacket and tear-away warm-up pants.

Peaches was overcome by the gifts, which were better than any Christmas morning surprises waiting under a tree. Merene hugged him as he cried. Barnabas drew him aside later, whispering something into his ear that visibly comforted the young man.

Diz yelped excitedly. A race-day uniform had been custom-made for the little dog, and he would don it with confidence tomorrow. When Peaches saw it, he was able to laugh through his tears.

Race morning came. Saturday was cold, cloudy, and windy. Incredibly windy. With its wicked elevation changes, the course lent itself to whirlwinds and gusts that would batter each runner differently as they navigated it. Cross-country was as much of a mental exercise as it was physical. In an endurance sport, it wasn't always the best athlete that crossed the finish line first. It was the person who remained tough and pushed and exhibited the greatest self-control through the duration. It was a punishing exercise in discipline and patience.

Barnabas and Diz stood with the team but at a distance. The pep talk before the race lineup was a good one.

"Ladies and gentlemen, we're not running for record times on a course like this. Pace yourself and place yourself. Save what you have and kick at the end, which will be uphill. Brady and the River Rats will be waiting for you!" The coach nodded to Barnabas, who revealed his matching race suit next to Diz.

The team died laughing. Their two biggest fans were a terrier and an ancient man who looked like he was in better shape than many of the racers.

"Brady will be waiting for you at the finish line," Barnabas had told Peaches the night before. "And I'll run the last mile with you."

As the contestants lined up, the announcers named each of them by school.

"From Novinger, Missouri, the Wild Cats, also known as the River Rats, led by Captain Jackson Peecher."

"Peaches!" the Novinger contingent screamed in unison.

Peaches had a pre-race routine that had never failed him. He closed his eyes and envisioned the finish line. He saw Merene, he saw Kenneth and Sharyn, and he saw Brady. Brady was so real Peaches forgot for a few seconds that he had died. In Peaches's vision, Brady wasn't bald and puffy and jaundiced and sick-looking. He had grown taller and had a full head of hair and was smiling and happy.

"Who is Jackson Peecher?" Brady asked playfully. "Your name is Peaches!"

With eyes closed, Peaches smiled until he heard the voice of Clayton "Business" Buys, who had sought him out to line up next to him.

"Nice uniform," Business said. "At least now you don't look like you're on welfare and shopping at the thrift store."

Peaches stared ahead, stone-faced and silent.

"Wait. Are you on welfare?" Business asked, taunting.

The announcer started a countdown to ten. The race would start with an airhorn blast.

"For Brady?" Business asked, reading the back of Peaches's uniform. "Why? He's dead."

Peaches lost his cool. He turned to stare down his rival right as the horn blasted.

Business left him behind, zipping forward like a mechanical rabbit at a greyhound track. Business was pleased. The sucker took the bait.

Infuriated, Peaches blistered after him. Peaches dodged and weaved through a pack of runners with ease as he caught up with Business, who was the clear front-runner.

The coach was immediately concerned. He saw the sprint and had seen the exchange between the two kids at the starting line. He was sure the pretty boy was a trash talker because Peaches certainly wasn't. The coach caught Peaches's attention near the one-mile mark. "Slow it down, hot shot! He can't beat you if you don't beat yourself!"

Business backed off at the mile marker, letting Peaches take a wide lead.

The air currents on the course were insane, ranging from dead stillness to violent, sidewinding gusts. The wind had been at the backs of the runners for the first mile, giving many false confidence. It took a wicked turn in the second mile, blowing straight in their faces.

Peaches didn't look behind, but he realized he was being stalked by a confident, able-bodied predator. He eased up, but he'd run too hot up until that point, as his lungs and calves protested. He knew he needed to save himself for the widow-maker hill looming ahead. He didn't like the feeling of losing the lead. He slowed his tempo as a small pack of a half dozen runners slipped past him.

Business overtook him near the final mile mark. Peaches knew he was in trouble. He closed his eyes.

"Don't chase him," Brady said. Peaches nodded as if the voice in his head were actually his departed little brother in the flesh. "Nice shoes!"

Peaches blinked a couple of times in delirium. He saw Barnabas at the base of the hill in the distance. The old man hadn't lied about running the final stretch. He was ready to sprint to the finish line with Peaches.

As Peaches approached the rise, he saw Business had already begun the ascent. He was fading; his pace shortened as his feet seemed to shuffle. He craned his head back, gasping for air, pulling up slightly, as if he had tweaked a muscle. He put his flashy gold chain in his mouth, holding it in place with his lips like a baby with a binky.

Diz was holding a portable stereo in his mouth. It caught Peaches's attention when it started blaring the hard-driving, bluesy "Rat Salad." In a brief half second, he looked over to see the dog sprinting up along the sideline. Barnabas Hassan, slim and athletic, ran ahead of him with his finger pointed toward the finish line at the top of the hill a short half mile ahead.

The clouds broke, revealing sunshine. In the newfound light, Peaches saw Merene waiting. And as sure as doubting Thomas saw the risen Christ, Peaches saw Brady standing next to her, jubilant and excited and jumping. He didn't look sick at all.

"I'm right here waiting for you," Brady's voice said. "Try to catch Mr. Hassan if you can. You can't even beat an old man!"

Peaches quickened his pace as he started the climb. The wind returned to his favor, pushing him along. He started a silent count to get his breathing and footsteps in rhythm. He could feel his legs coming alive with speed as his lungs burned. Down to the last quarter of a mile.

Peaches didn't see it but felt it when he passed Business.

"Take that, punk!" Brady yelled.

A surly cross breeze blew, pushing Business slightly off course. Peaches ran into the wind like a linebacker bracing himself for a tackle.

He heard Barnabas's voice to his left. "You're almost there!"

One lone spectator had managed to fix his gaze not on the oncoming runners but on the outlandish duo of a uniformed old man sprinting with his uniformed dog—a baffling sight. "Damn," the random onlooker said out loud. "That grandpa is haulin' ass!"

Piercing through the dull roar of the crowd at the finish line, Merene's voice sounded in Peaches's ears. "I love you!" she yelled.

He closed his eyes in the final stretch.

When he woke up, he found himself flat on his back a few stumbles past the finish line.

"I'm so proud of you!" Brady said, standing over his brother.

The announcer barked excitedly, egged on by excited barking from Diz. "Ladies and gentlemen! Your Missouri State High School Activities Association cross-country state champion! Novinger's Jackson 'Peaches' Peecher!"

"Brady!" the crowds screamed. "Brady!"

Brady grinned. Peaches blinked. Brady disappeared.

Merene found Peaches and hugged him, emotionally exhausted. She had her hair in a single rattail braid with red-and-white ribbons. She had never looked prettier to Peaches than she did that day. Her golden-flecked green eyes were glassy with tears. She kissed him, realizing the whole town was watching the two of them.

"He was here with us, Peaches," she said. "Brady was standing next to me; I swear to God. He wasn't sick anymore, and he told me to tell you he was proud of you."

Diz, in his matching race suit, still held the portable stereo in his mouth. Barnabas, looking spry, sauntered over to the state champion, who had gotten to his feet. Both the old man and the new state champion were out of breath.

"Where is he?" Peaches asked.

Peaches knew Barnabas had seen Brady. As Barnabas had dashed toward the finish, he'd pointed toward him at the finish line.

After catching his breath, Barnabas replied with a single word: "paradise."

Peaches was crushed yet relieved, and Barnabas held him as he sobbed on his shoulder. Touched by the occasion, Merene joined in a three-way hug with Kenneth and Sharyn, who laughed and cried.

Later in the day, Clayton "Business" Buys stood emotionless at the awards ceremony, feeling terrible about himself, not because he had lost the state championship but because he realized heckling someone about their dead kid brother was a regret he would carry for the rest of his life. But, even in the depths of his sincere remorse, Business lacked the courage to congratulate or apologize to the victor.

How the mighty fall.

Peaches made the front-page news of the Saint Louis Post-Dispatch under a headline that read simply, "For Brady." Merene considered clipping the article to send to Business but thought better of it after talking with Barnabas—and Diz.

"Should I send it, Diz?" she asked.

He shook his head, barking vigorously.

# CHAPTER TWENTY

It was New Year's Eve. Peaches decided he and Merene would enjoy a wild night of partying by playing dominoes with Kenneth, Sharyn, and Barnabas. Sharyn made a big pot of beans and cornbread. They whiled the night away together as a New Year's morning came. The revelers stepped out onto the porch to light some fireworks to celebrate. Merene rested her head on Peaches's shoulder as they held hands. He knew she was worried about him.

Later that week, Peaches would be headed to Fort Benning, Georgia, for basic training and military occupational specialty training as a combat medic specialist. He felt guilty that he would be leaving her behind. She would be alone for their senior prom in the spring. He would also miss the commencement ceremony, having finished a semester early.

"You better come home to me. That's all I'm asking for."

Eavesdropping, Barnabas spoke up. "He'll come home."

Merene sniffled as she fanned her eyes, concentrating on the pop-whiz-bang and bright colors of the fireworks to distract her from her sadness. "How can you say that? How do you know?"

Barnabas, looking regal, touched his hand to his chin as if to stroke a beard he didn't have. "I'm an old man." He folded his hands as if praying and looked up at the stars in the clear night sky. "We've talked about it. He'll come home."

They would all miss Peaches, especially Kenneth. Peaches was a big help to him on the farm. Merene planned to help out when she wasn't busy at the Glastonbury Market or with school activities.

New Year's Day came and went. Days later, Peaches found himself saying goodbye to his parents. His mother, gaunt and reeking of cigarette smoke, cried like a baby as she saw her son off. His father wouldn't come to the house. Peaches went to the shop, where his father stood with a beer in hand, smoking. Three empties lay at his feet. It was five thirty in the morning. He had started early.

"You've done well, young man, despite having a sorry-ass son of a bitch for a father."

Peaches snorted, brushing off the deprecation. The elder Peecher extended his hand to his son. "You're a man now."

Looking through the shop's open metal roll-up doors at the morning, the father imparted a single line of advice while keeping his son at an awkward distance. "Don't turn out like me."

Peaches held a firm grip on his father's hand and squeezed. He felt like a hug was in order, but his father was not the hugging type. The compliments and his own self-loathing were the best the emotionally absent man could muster.

Walking to Merene's car, where she was waiting to drive him to the airport in Saint Louis, he had a premonition that he wouldn't see his old man again.

The three hours to Saint Louis flew by as the two enjoyed each other's company. They laughed as every other song on the radio seemed to be by the rapper Nelly, who happened to be from Saint Louis. His most popular song had a repetitive chorus about it being hot and taking clothes off because of it.

"You'll be singing about how it's hot every day and missing the snow in Missouri," Merene said. The pair was convinced Peaches would be deployed to somewhere hot like the Middle East.

"I don't think I'll ever miss the cold. Just you," Peaches said.

The couple stopped for lunch at Imo's, an iconic pizzeria serving authentic, Saint-Louis style pies. The crust was thin and crispy like a cracker, and instead of wedge-shaped slices, the pizzas were cut into squares. The cheese was some secret proprietary variety that was creamier and meltier than anything they had tried before.

"Maybe we should move to Saint Louis when you come home," Merene said. Thinking about the future was a welcome distraction from the thought of the goodbye looming at the airport.

Peaches shook his head. "It's a cult, Merene. It's a cult." He scanned the crowd in the pizzeria, leaning forward as he picked out "cult" members and raising his eyebrows.

Saint Louis Cardinals fans were so devoted to their hometown baseball team it was almost a religion. Merene realized the two looked out of place because they lacked Cardinals T-shirts or caps.

Then they made their way to another iconic Saint Louis fixture, Ted Drewes Frozen Custard, which, strangely enough, was also well-known for selling Christmas trees for the holidays.

"They weren't lying!" Peaches exclaimed as he held his malt upside down. The Ted Drewes logo was an upside-down cup. Their shakes and malts were so thick they defied gravity by staying in place when overturned. The frozen custard worked like a charm, curing the pair's depression one creamy mouthful at a time.

Eventually, they parked the car and entered the concourse of the Lambert Field airport, which was larger and more populous than Novinger by untold multiples. Merene promised herself she wouldn't cry. She didn't want to be that stereotypical, woe-is-me, weeping mess. She hugged Peaches, and they held each other for a long time. It seemed like time stood still in the midst of the busy hub.

She heard Barnabas's voice in her head. "He'll come home." She swore she saw him and Diz off in the distance. When she looked again, they had vanished. It must've been her mind playing tricks on her.

"I love you," she said and kissed Peaches on the cheek.

Peaches was quiet for an uncomfortable amount of time. "I know."

"I'm about ready to punch you, jerk face!"

"I love you too."

"I know." Merene squeezed Peaches tight and leaned in to whisper in his ear. "'Go forth and set the world on fire.'" The quote was famously attributed, or maybe misattributed, to the soldier-turned-priest Ignatius Loyola.

When Merene turned around to leave, she thought she saw Barnabas and Diz again.

When she blinked—as before—they disappeared.

# CHAPTER TWENTY-ONE

Peaches soon discovered that he both loved and hated the military.

Basic training, at least the physical fitness portion, was a cinch. He found himself running laps around the base in the evenings to maintain his long-standing fifty-to-seventy-mile-a-week running habit.

Recruits woke up at four thirty a.m., dressed, passed a room inspection, and then proceeded to eat at the mess hall. The food wasn't as bad as in the stories he had heard. Or maybe it was just that he wasn't very picky. Physical fitness and drills lasted a couple of hours, followed by instruction in military doctrine, the history of the army, and principles of combat.

Peaches became "Peecher" overnight, which was strange. Recruits were called, or maybe more accurately barked at, by their last names. What Peaches didn't like was the do-as-I-say-without-question nature of officers. He found his drill instructor to be a hard-ass but no more intimidating than what years of living with a raging alcoholic father had been. He sensed that his drill instructor resented the fact that he wasn't scared of him.

Recruits learned "LDRSHIP"—a mnemonic for the core values of loyalty, duty, respect, selfless service, honor, integrity, and personal courage. They had little time for chitchat and relaxation, except for an hour or two after supper when recruits could exercise, study, read, or write letters home.

"We like the same book," a recruit named Jarju said to Peaches one evening, gesturing to Peaches's copy of the Koran.

Jarju's nickname was Jar Jar, like the Star Wars character. He was always cheerful and effervescent. The guy was a living, breathing pick-me-up. Jar Jar was from a tiny country in West Africa called The Gambia, which Peaches probably wouldn't be able to find on a map to save his life. Jar Jar wasn't yet a US citizen but had a green card and would gain citizenship sometime during his military service. Regardless, he was immensely proud to wear his US Army uniform.

Peaches had brought a copy of the Koran to basic training after reading that both Napoleon and General Patton had been known to study the holy book at length. He watched as Jar Jar did the same prayer routine every evening. He raised his palms to his ears, signifying the greatness of God. He then bowed on the floor, prostrate, praying.

"You know most people don't realize that Christians and Jews and Muslims worship the same God. We're basically spiritual cousins," Jar Jar said.

Peaches learned that the Prophet Muhammad had frequently mentioned that Jesus and Moses and Abraham were among the righteous, serving one almighty God. The stark difference between Muslims and Christians was whether a person believed that Jesus was divine.

"I'll ask him someday in heaven," Jar Jar said, winking at Peaches.

A bond of friendship grew between them with each boot-camp day checked off the calendar. Peaches was selected as platoon leader in his recruit class by the drill instructor, narrowly edging out Jar Jar. Gracious in defeat, he would assist him as the second recruit in command of the marches and drills. "It's God's will," he said. "Congratulations, sir."

Peaches wrote to Merene every day. "I started playing soccer, or football. It's really an impressive sport. Jar Jar calls it 'the beautiful game.'"

"Americans think American football is a big deal," Jar Jar said. "Which it is, but only in America. Millions of people play it. Real football is played everywhere in the world by billions. Think about that."

Peaches didn't yet understand all the rules but grasped the basics of offense, defense, and not ever using your hands to touch the ball. It was a good workout. A soccer player ran nonstop. The conditioning required to run for forty-five minutes or an hour at once was no different from cross-country.

Jar Jar was an exceptional football player. He commanded the field like a general, barking out orders to others to set them up where he needed them to be.

He shouted at Peaches in frustration. "Just run and get me the ball. Okay?"

Peaches quickly found himself looking up at the bright blue sky.

"You're fine," Jar Jar said. He extended his hand to a flummoxed Peaches. He'd unintentionally laid him out flat on his back as they practiced ball-handling skills in their free time. "Get up!"

Peaches found the running easy but the fancy footwork required to dribble the ball challenging. He thought, foolishly, that soccer was a passive, non-contact sport. Eleven-on-eleven football (the kind with the round ball) was far from non-contact. Players constantly crashed into one another incidentally. Jar Jar used his powerful hips and thighs to angle for possession of the ball, sometimes tossing opponents to the ground, in a move reminiscent of a judo throw. He was a different person on the soccer field, akin to a Roman gladiator. And to top it all off, he played without wearing socks or shoes.

"What?" Jar Jar asked Peaches, looking at him the first time they played in the evening. "You're a cornbread hillbilly, man. You grew up barefoot too!"

Outside of The Gambian capital city of Banjul, where Jar Jar was raised, kids gathered in dirt lots to play football, whether they had shoes or not. That was the universal appeal of the beautiful game. It could be played anytime, anywhere, with minimal equipment. All that was needed was a flat spot, a ball, and strong lungs.

Peaches, normally not a worrier, worried when their drill instructor decided he wanted to play in one of their pickup games.

"Don't cut him any slack. We play to win," Jar Jar said.

Fighting for a stolen pass, Jar Jar crashed into the stern man, sending him reeling. Unfazed, he offered a hand, helping him to his feet. He then voluntarily pumped out fifty rapid-fire push-ups before going back to the game.

"Sir, my apologies, sir."

The instructor brushed it off. "Jarju, you're tough. Well done. Give me another set."

Jar Jar did as he was told, his arms and chest burning from the repetitions. Then, out of breath, he hollered at his fellow platoon members watching in shock. "Back to ball. Let's go!"

The drill instructor's team ended up losing the match.

Peaches and Jar Jar led their recruit platoon as they posted colors during basic training graduation, in front of hundreds of friends, family, and military brass assembled to congratulate the freshly minted soldiers. They felt good in a uniform, and it showed.

Not only had they become the best of friends, but they shared the same training as medics. Each had excelled in large part to the credit of the other, like the old "iron sharpens iron" analogy. Their cohort would soon be dispatched around the world—many headed to Iraq. Just a couple of years removed from the fall of the Twin Towers, Peaches and Jar Jar received special orders for Arizona.

"You're heading to Fort Huachuca," their commander said. "Military intelligence training on special assignment."

# CHAPTER TWENTY-TWO

It was unusual but not completely unheard of to have a secondary training specialty.

The US Army Intelligence Center of Excellence was located less than twenty miles from Mexico in the Sonoran Desert. Huachuca had a storied past, starting out as a simple campsite as the US Army fought the Apache, eventually forcing the famed fighting Chief Geronimo to a surrender in 1886. The Huachuca Mountains surrounded the enclave. It never really got terribly hot, or at least it never felt that way, due to the dry desert air. Peaches and Jar Jar were surprised to find out how cool the nights were.

"God, I miss cornfields," Peaches said, half in jest and half-truthfully.

The starkness of the arid outpost was difficult for both young men to adjust to. The area received the bulk of its few annual inches of moisture during July and August. Violent, torrential rain seemed to slap and batter the timid, parched land. After the rain came and left, the desert, albeit briefly, bloomed in a magnificent show of color.

"I wish I could send you pictures," Peaches wrote to Merene. "Sharyn would love this." Detailed letters and calls were highly restricted, given the sensitive nature of military intelligence.

Peaches and Jar Jar had settled in at Fort Huachuca and stayed there for nearly a year before they received orders. They had plenty of good times training, hiking and camping in the desert mountains, learning to pilot drones to gather intelligence, and scoping out secret hideouts. Though they hadn't yet seen combat injuries, they had already saved a life.

A soldier was thrown from an ATV in a remote canyon, part of a seek-and-destroy training mission in which small dispatches of soldiers were dropped with orders to take out an encampment and return to base camp as soon as possible. Peaches and Jar Jar were embedded with the attacking drill team. Though it was simulated, live fire and improvised explosive devices—IEDs—were everywhere. Raiders flew specialized drones to try to detect the slightest indentations in the arid earth to pinpoint the spots where the homemade bombs lay in wait.

Simulated radio chatter for the "enemy" was in a strange foreign tongue.

Jar Jar shook his head. "When we're done Boy Scouting, I bet they'll send us to Afghanistan."

Peaches didn't think so. He had read how the violent and zealous Taliban regime had been toppled by the US and how the new Afghan government was trying to bring order to one of the poorest, most desolate countries in the world.

During their drill, the team camped out in the desert, making shallow, makeshift dugouts to avoid detection. One of their team members had discovered a rival compound with a small surveillance drone. It identified several personnel in a remote, rocky outpost outfitted with AKs mounted on pedestals that looked like they'd been welded together by drunken Missouri hillbillies. It was very similar to what soldiers would encounter in field conditions during live combat. The enemy in real life was trained to take no prisoners, nor would they allow themselves to be taken prisoner. A living terrorist was a very valuable asset for the United States military, if they could be acquired.

After leaving the simulated enemy compound seemingly undetected, a retreating soldier heard the sickening hum of an unfriendly drone overhead. Rather than risk a firefight, the soldier escaped down a canyon pass on foot until he reached his waiting dirt bike. As he started up the lightweight, demonically fast Japanese motorcycle, he heard the hum of more drones. It jarred the young man as he made a run for it.

The desert was dark and quiet and eerily still. A small rock caught the bike's front wheel, hurling its rider. The soldier was quite seriously injured. He radioed for medics immediately. The launch from the bike had sliced open a vein in his left arm.

"I can feel my own blood gushing over me."

"Hold on. We're coming," Peaches said.

They traveled to him on foot. The canyons where the young man had been thrown were too treacherous for vehicular traffic. The enemy drones circled, trying to pinpoint the young man, who was bleeding out. He had crawled into a shallow arroyo carved out by the flooding desert rainwaters. Jar Jar shot a few tracer bullets in the air, catching the attention of the drones. They were distracted momentarily and changed course, looking for the unseen combatant. Even though this wasn't a real-life battlefield, it had very real consequences.

Peaches ran fast that night. The high altitude and rough terrain of the Huachuca Mountains had strengthened his heart and lungs like those world-class distance runners training up among the clouds in their mountain homelands.

Peaches found the injured soldier in bad shape. His pulse was racing wildly, and his breathing was shallow. Talking to himself out loud helped Peaches to stay focused on his patient. "Brachial artery. Severe vascular injury to the upper extremity."

The man needed to be triaged and would need surgery as soon as possible back at the base. A rock had sliced through his upper arm when he was vaulted from his motorbike. The open wound looked like a raw ribeye steak in the moonlight.

"Penetrating trauma." Peaches took off a boot and removed one of his socks. The bandages in his pack were not strong enough to make the tourniquet he had diagrammed in his mind during the past few seconds. He used his teeth to rip through the soldier's bloodied uniform to bare enough skin so that he could implement the impromptu medical device. He applied pressure and stopped the bleeding, which was crucial. Plenty of the patient's blood had already flowed out before he got there. It gathered in a sickening puddle.

The soldier's teeth were chattering from shock. Peaches knew he and Jar Jar would need to race the young man back as fast as possible. "Come to me!" Peaches yelled out loud.

"Engage," a commander radioed to Jar Jar.

He shot directly at the enemy drone swarm, hitting a few.

"Uncle Sam won't like that! Those are expensive!" Peaches shouted.

Jar Jar arrived, and they carried the soldier back. The exercise had been called off to rush the ailing man to the base's hospital. Peaches and Jar Jar rode with their patient on a Jeep as they wound through the rough terrain. They rushed into the hospital, where the army surgeon was waiting with a team ready to get to work. The young men were allowed to wait outside of the operating room. Peaches closed his eyes. Jar Jar was praying.

Peaches saw Diz as his eyelids slid shut. The image of the dog was comforting. Peaches was still dreaming. Diz smiled and spoke in a human voice. "You saved his life."

He opened his eyes in shock.

The doctor emerged from the operating room, removing his surgical mask. "You saved his life. Or I should say, your sock saved his life."

Relieved, Peaches threw his arms around the surgeon in a celebratory embrace. The doctor was surprised at the outpouring of emotion.

Jar Jar approached Peaches and did the same, adding a few congratulatory backslaps to the mix. "Good work, soldier!" Jar Jar whispered into his ear.

As they left the hospital, Peaches thought he saw a dog scampering around the corner. "Diz?"

"Who is Diz?" Jar Jar asked.

"You just wouldn't believe me if I told you."

"Try me."

"It's my elderly neighbor's dog from back home. I had this vision of him, and he told me I saved that guy's life just before the doctor confirmed it."

"Lord! Dogs can speak in Missouri?" Jar Jar smiled, and his exposed teeth gleamed in the moonlight before he cackled. "We need to take you back to get your head checked!"

# CHAPTER TWENTY-THREE

Merene settled into a comfortable routine in Peaches's absence. It was archaic and old-fashioned, but she really liked reading and writing letters. There was something genuine and sincere and earnest about having to sit down with pen and paper to write out her thoughts, a sort of relic from a lost time. Perhaps she'd picked it up from Barnabas.

An expert in antiquity, Barnabas was a prolific letter-writer. He wasn't much for modern conveniences like email. He had a personal library and study, which Peaches had been to, describing it to Merene only as "a wonder." Merene couldn't possibly believe it could be so, since his cottage house was small and plain and unimpressive.

In his absence, it didn't take long for Merene to realize how much Peaches did for his parents, which strengthened her love for him. Peaches's dad had been on military disability benefits for as long as Merene could remember, though he did odd jobs fabricating parts for machines and custom mods for hot rods and classic cars. But Peaches paid the electricity and propane bills and made sure their vehicles had enough gas. As the only one who acted like a parent in the household, Peaches had to remind his parents to tell him when they needed necessities like socks and underwear. He bought what little groceries they needed that weren't in a bottle. Peaches never bought his parents alcohol, though it was common for kids in the country to pick up booze and cigarettes for their parents while store clerks looked the other way. Merene, naturally, didn't allow this to happen at the Glastonbury Market. She ran a tight ship.

She made it a habit to stop by the Peecher house in the morning, where she was usually greeted by Mrs. Peecher breakfasting on cigarettes and black coffee. Mr. Peecher had a cot out in his shop where he stayed most nights, passing out after he finished his nightly case of beer. Mrs. Peecher didn't drive, so Merene would take her to Kirksville on occasion for doctors' appointments or to shop.

Merene found that she had fallen right back into the role of being a parent to a parent. But this time, it wasn't as painful. Caring for Mrs. Peecher helped to ease the pain of her mother's absence. She accidentally called Peaches's mother "mom" when they were out doing errands together one day. When she saw Mrs. Peecher's eyes fill with tears, Merene's eyes followed suit. She realized that by caring for Mrs. Peecher, her love for Peaches grew, despite the distance between them. If only she could connect with Mr. Peecher, Merene thought. He remained as cold and distant and isolated as ever.

Merene operated on autopilot for the last semester of her senior year. She participated in a work-study program in which she received credit for working at the Glastonbury Market half of the day. She had one legitimate academic class, which happened to be an English course through the local community college in Kirksville. The instructor was a trip, a goofy, rambling free spirit who liked to read.

"Let's talk about books," the instructor said, sitting cross-legged on the floor. "You don't have to worry about homework. You'll write a paper at the end of the semester. Just turn it in whenever you get to it."

Merene was diligent in keeping up with the required readings, which she found interesting. She liked to discuss her assignments with Barnabas, who seemed to have read every book ever written. He had a way of looking off into the distance, reminiscing. Merene jokingly called it the "thousand-mile stare."

"Tell me about the Miners' Ball," she said to him one day.

He paused while sipping his coffee at the market as he made his usual morning rounds. His eyes lit up. "They were wonderful."

Kenneth chimed in. "Perry Como came one year. The Perry Como came to little ole Novinger."

Diz barked and jumped then pushed his nose into Kenneth's pant leg.

"I think Diz is reminding me that Bob Wills came, too, all the way from Texas."

Diz nodded and wagged his tail.

"Who is Perry Como? And Bob Wills?" Merene asked. She saw a look of disgust on Kenneth's face. "Sorry. They probably were great, but I've never heard of them."

Still staring, as if living a past moment all over again, Barnabas spoke. He seemed at a loss for words. "I could never... I could never express enough of my appreciation for the men and women who worked the mines all those years."

Merene had heard the Cinderella-like stories of the balls before. The Glastonbury Company had seamstresses brought in from Kansas City and Saint Louis to custom tailor new suits for the miners and new dresses for their wives.

"Everybody felt like a somebody," Kenneth said. "And Barnabas here was no goody-two-shoes Methodist. He could dance!"

"You could too," Barnabas said.

"Really?" Merene asked, surprised.

"Well, well. It only took a couple thousand years of life on earth, but this man has finally told his first lie!" Kenneth said. Kenneth Love was born with two left feet.

"Do you remember the horses and mules?" Barnabas asked.

Sharyn had been poking around the market, listening in on the talk of old times, and she interjected herself into the reminiscences. "I reckon they looked prettier than some of the men!" The horses and mules that pulled coal carts deep underground were outfitted for the ball to pull carriages full of attendees. They were groomed and bridled for the event, looking slicker and more impressive than the Budweiser Clydesdales.

"We should hold a Miners' Ball again," Merene said.

"We should," Barnabas said.

Diz concurred with a bark.

Merene had become the social director of sorts for her senior class, leading the yearbook committee and planning their prom, which was set for May, just a few weeks before graduation. The idea for the prom, honestly, came to her in a dream, a recollection of a conversation she had had with Peaches.

"You should see his library," Peaches's voice had said in the dream. Barnabas's personal library and study had to be in the old mine. There was no way his tiny house could contain such a purportedly voluminous collection of materials. "It's a wonder. They used to have formal dances down there in the old days with a big band and flappers and probably bootleg liquor."

On the fly, Merene asked Barnabas, Sadie Hawkins-style. "Will you be my prom date?"

Kenneth whistled.

"Poor Peaches hasn't been gone but a few months and you're already chasing after older men!"

# CHAPTER TWENTY-FOUR

Merene had lived in Novinger her entire life, yet she had never been inside the Glastonbury Mine. It closed and shuttered long before she was born in the 1980s. She walked with Barnabas, Diz, and Sharyn along a path leading to the entrance. With spring coming, Kenneth was busy on his tractor, getting the fields ready for planting, and couldn't join them.

A manicured stone monument sign reading "Glastonbury" was surrounded by hawthorns. The side entrance was sealed off from unwanted guests by a giant boulder. It reminded Merene of Easter pageants she had participated in as a child, in which an angel greeted the women coming to take care of Christ's crucified body in the tomb provided by the kindly Joseph of Arimathea. The mine's main entrance consisted of two half-moon-shaped doors that slid together.

"This brings back some memories," Sharyn said. "I used to make lunches and bring them to the mine when I was your age."

Barnabas reached for a light switch after he slid open the doors. Merene had unconsciously grabbed Sharyn's hand, halfway expecting a jump scare from some long-forgotten zombie who was certain to leap out from the darkness. The switch was more of a lever looking like something from a Frankenstein movie. The lights came on with a warm, soft glow. The entryway was clean, with a path leading to an elevator. There was also a lookout office, where miners had checked in and out throughout their day's work.

"Does the elevator work?" Merene asked.

"I guess we're about to find out," Barnabas said.

Sharyn hooted. "Don't scare the poor girl!"

Merene clenched Sharyn's hand as they stepped into the elevator, which was large enough to comfortably hold a dozen people. Its metal doors closed like a clamshell.

As their tour guide, Barnabas began explaining. "The Glastonbury produced high-quality coal, which means it had low amounts of sulfur."

The elevator rattled and shook as they descended.

"There are ten stopes, each about one hundred feet above one another. A stope is an old English term for a dugout. The deepest stope in the mine is almost a thousand feet underground."

The clamshell doors opened to a pit of blackness.

Merene gasped. "Oh God."

Barnabas whistled. "Let's hope the elevator works going up!"

"Stop it!" Sharyn said.

Barnabas reached to the right as they stepped out into total darkness. He flipped another switch, which seemed to set off a chain reaction of lights illuminating cavernous rooms in the mine.

"Wow!" Merene exclaimed.

Diz barked, and it echoed, reverberating throughout the underground fortress. The mine was laid out in an orderly fashion with main walkways and carveouts channeling off like driveways along a country road.

"Rooms and pillars," Barnabas said. "The men had to be very careful to leave enough supports as they excavated. Thankfully, we never had collapses. As the coal was mined, it was crushed and then fed into a belt system that carried it upward to carts. The carts were pulled by mules and horses in the old days and then eventually replaced by machines."

"This could be a hotel!" Merene said.

The ceilings were probably fifteen feet tall.

"Do you think it'll be big enough for your dance?"

There must have been ten football fields worth of rooms and pillars.

"You could fit the entire city underground."

Merene found the mine less intimidating and more fascinating with each passing moment. "People could have shops down here, and you could easily put in restaurants and hotel rooms," she said, thinking out loud. "Why go to the tourist traps in Branson when you could come here?"

Diz barked in agreement.

"This is going to be awesome." She hugged Barnabas. "Thank you."

"You know, he's quite the dancer," Sharyn said.

"Was," Barnabas said. "In my younger years."

In her excitement, Merene had forgotten to ask to see the library, which had to be down there somewhere.

The prom would be on a Friday evening, followed by a Saturday evening Miners' Ball for the entire community. Barnabas would take care of the arrangements and musical entertainment for both events. "I'm afraid Perry Como won't make this Miners' Ball," he said. Mr. Como had passed away a couple of years before. "But we'll make it memorable."

Merene thought of her mother and how she and Barnabas, oddly enough, shared a fondness for the Allman Brothers. It felt like she was there with them.

"I still haven't seen the library. I know it's down there somewhere," Merene wrote to Peaches.

"It's worth the wait" was Peaches's only reply on the subject.

"I wish you were here for prom and the Miners' Ball, but I'm taking Barnabas. He'll dance, and I know you won't."

Peaches grinned and laughed out loud as he read Merene's letter. She was right.

"Sharyn says he's a good dancer too."

Merene had signed off "Love you" on her letters to Peaches. It was kind of funny, considering they weren't lovey-dovey people.

"I love me too," Peaches had written when concluding his first reply letter to Merene during basic training. He finally relented on a future letter with "Love you more."

Merene cried when she read it out loud.

# CHAPTER TWENTY-FIVE

What Merene didn't write to tell Peaches was how much she worried about his dad. He was an angry, broken man who drank like a fish and smoked like a forest fire. This wasn't news to Peaches, but Merene couldn't see how his father could possibly live long abusing his body the way he did.

She felt a growing connection to his mother. She would hold Merene's hand and gently pat it in thanks as Merene dropped her off at home from her appointments or after they returned from shopping.

Merene had spent a lot of time with Barnabas since Peaches left. He wanted to make sure she was getting the most out of her work-study arrangement for school. The man was unfathomably wise, patient, and perceptive. He showed Merene his ledger books, which he used to account for the revenues and expenses of the Glastonbury Market and for the dozens of properties he owned. Almost half of Novinger was delinquent on their monthly grocery tabs. Merene wondered what would have become of the town had Barnabas abandoned them when the mines closed after the fire. It probably would have shriveled and died and turned to dust and blown away in the wind.

Merene helped Kenneth with the profit and loss financial reports for the volunteer fire department and, like Peaches had done before her, joined the group to pursue training as a paramedic. She aced the emergency medical technician (EMT) exam in record time and studied a bit every day for board examinations for paramedic certification.

A few weeks later, Merene stood in front of a full-length mirror in a dress shop on Kirksville's historic town square.

"Young 'un," Sharyn said, "you look gorgeous."

The chiffon dress was perfect, its deep scarlet contrasted by white lace hawthorn flowers on the top.

"You won't have to worry about Barnabas. He knows how to dress," Sharyn said.

He would wear a white suit. For fun, Merene would wear a matching porkpie hat, the same style she had seen the old man don often. Merene felt good, and she knew she looked good by the glances sent her way from other customers in the formal wear shop.

"It's perfect. I just wish my mother could see me."

Barnabas quietly paid for all the dresses and the tailoring for Merene and her classmates. While he was amused to be invited to the prom, he was really looking forward to the Miners' Ball the following evening.

Kenneth barreled out of a dressing room, seeing Merene in her outfit for the first time. "Pretty, pretty, but not as pretty as me." He looked at himself in the mirror as Merene did the same.

"Kenneth, you clean up good. I figured you'd just wear clean overalls to the ball!"

"I was informed that wasn't an option. Mother," Kenneth said, looking toward Sharyn, "did you make an appointment for me to get my hair did like Merene?"

"What hair?"

Kenneth rubbed the top of his head, not encountering much resistance.

Sharyn booked the best hairdresser in Kirksville for Merene to get a cut, wash, color, and style the Friday morning of the prom. Merene, Sharyn, and her classmates spent the Thursday afternoon before decorating.

Barnabas had booked a photo booth. There was a thirty-second delay before the camera flash went off. He found a lot of old mining props—shovels, pickaxes, belts, helmets with headlamps, old dynamite cases, and so on—to use. It would be fun. He had also hired a professional photographer to take pictures suitable for framing.

The man thought of everything. Huge cooling towers were brought in to make sure the long-abandoned mine would remain comfortable for the dancers both for the Friday prom and for the Miners' Ball on Saturday. Professional musicians from the Saint Louis Symphony Orchestra would be playing live at both events. A DJ was booked for those who enjoyed more modern music.

The cavernous rooms where the dances were going to be held were surprisingly clean and dust-free. It looked like the walls and pillars had been sprayed down with some sort of lacquer. All the areas where people would walk, dance, or sit had been covered by portable flooring. Even temporary restrooms, with running water, electricity, and speakers inside, had been delivered. Minus the pitch-black darkness beyond, a person wouldn't have known they were in an abandoned coal mine.

"Look at this," Merene said, amazed. "People would come from miles around to have this experience. We could have a museum and a bed-and-breakfast and shops and special events, all right beneath Novinger. People could have weddings and receptions here."

"How about a movie theater?" Kenneth asked, in jest.

"Why not?"

# CHAPTER TWENTY-SIX

Merene clipped out the article from the Saint Louis Post-Dispatch.

"Subterranean Shindig," it read. The picture of the formal dance didn't do it justice.

"It was just amazing," Peaches read, noticing the capital letters and two underlines Merene had added for emphasis.

"Barnabas wanted no mention of himself," she wrote. When the reporters pressed for further information, the only revelation he was willing to divulge was that the Glastonbury Company was privileged to support the Novinger community.

"You might think I'm crazy, but I'm telling you the mine could be a tourist attraction someday," she wrote. "People crave one-of-a-kind experiences. We could put Novinger on the map."

Kenneth found it hilarious that the Miners' Ball was held in the mine. In the coal days, every worker dreamed of the whistle that would bring them out of the darkness at the end of their shift. Now, it seemed as if the tide had turned, with the gathered people of Novinger clamoring to head deep underground once again. But this time, they didn't look forward to leaving.

Merene finished up her recollection on a somber note. "He hasn't shown me his library yet, and I don't quite know how to ask to see it without being pushy... Peaches—the man can dance like you wouldn't believe." She underlined "believe" three times and dotted the pen point a few times above the word, the best approximation for celebratory confetti she could sketch.

The orchestra for the prom had been really wonderful, playing sophisticated songs for slow dancing. Barnabas was regal, refined, and measured on the dance floor. He danced a waltz with Merene, and that was when she realized something was really off.

The man's feet were light and airy. He almost floated across the portable dance flooring. She could tell he loved music. She began to doubt—in a deep and confusing way—that Barnabas Hassan was an old man at all. Merene pushed the thought out of her head. She didn't want mindless paranoia to ruin one of the best evenings of her life.

It's his positive attitude that makes him ageless, she reassured herself.

"Barnabas," Merene said, "you get to pick the last song."

Her voice echoed. The Miners' Ball had wrapped up. Novinger had never seen a better dance and celebration. The prom the evening before might have been a close second, but the Miners' Ball had three or four times the turnout.

"That's very kind of you," he said.

Saturday evening had turned into Sunday morning. The orchestra that played for the Miners' Ball had left hours ago, tipped generously by Barnabas. The disc jockey, all the way from Kansas City, had headed to a hotel room in Kirksville, a generosity Barnabas had insisted he oblige. He would retrieve his accoutrements in the morning.

"How about some long-hair music?" Barnabas said, imitating Kenneth.

Merene surveyed the DJ's equipment left behind, typing "Allman Brothers" on a screen.

"Ramblin' Man" was the first song that popped up, followed by "Jessica" and "Whipping Post."

Merene had thought of Teresa throughout the evening, wishing she had been there, so it seemed fitting to play something by the Allman Brothers.

A flitting click-click of the mouse queued "Ramblin' Man". A familiar, twangy guitar harmony filled the entire mine stope, one thousand feet below the earth.

Barnabas extended his hand to Merene as the instrumental intro was about to conclude. Barnabas sang along to the first few lyrics. Merene joined him. She had sung the song a thousand times with her mother. Barnabas couldn't restrain himself. The music seemed to electrify his body.

He popped his shoulders from side to side, in sync with the beat. His feet slid along the dance floor as if his shoes had been slicked down by a quick spritz of an aerosol lubricant. He twirled Merene and dipped her gently like Fred Astaire had done to Ginger Rogers long ago. She felt the twitching strength of his forearms and shoulders. He was no doddering geriatric.

He scooped her upright, unable to hide his sheer, exuberant joy. Then the song meandered to the middle part, instrumental and guitar-laden. They separated and did their own routines, lost in the music.

She closed her eyes, laughing and then crying the happiest of tears. She felt like somehow, telepathically, Barnabas had engineered this ensemble for Teresa. They were dancing for her, uninhibited. Merene engaged in rapid-fire blinking to contain the tears as best she could. Though the ball was long over, she didn't want to make a mess of her makeup.

Barnabas shimmied so swiftly the prom-goers last night would have been both jealous and amazed.

"Showin' off!" Kenneth said, his voice echoing.

Merene's gaze searched for its source but didn't find him. She went back to juking and jiving. Barnabas paused briefly and then clapped his hands as the guitar went wild in the song's crescendo. Merene clapped, too, pleased with the performance.

Diz emerged from the shadows. The little dog stared his master down, as if challenging him to a duel.

"You think so, Diz?" Barnabas said.

Stretching his front limbs out like a playing puppy, Diz bolted upright. He leapt into the air and landed a perfect backflip.

Kenneth and Sharyn, who had been somewhere in a different coal chamber, finishing up the removal of decorations and readying to head home, revealed themselves now, clapping. Kenneth yelled to Barnabas, "Top that, old man!"

Barnabas accepted the challenge. He shoulder-shrugged and placed his feet one in front of the other, like a death-defying tightrope walker working without the safety of a net below. His arms were tucked behind him, his chin up, his neck craned forward like one of those naked mermaid figureheads on ancient wooden sea ships. His knees were ever-so-slightly bent.

"Go on," Sharyn said. She was swaying gently back and forth, having a good time taking it all in.

Her voice startled Merene, who turned to look at her.

Clack-clack.

Merene whipped her gaze back to Barnabas, who was in nearly the same position he had been a moment before. His head tilted to one side. His hands were outstretched on either side of his body, as if he had completed a sleight-of-hand magic trick, holding still for dramatic embellishment, steadied for due admiration. He stood frozen in place.

Diz, in defeat, lay down on his back, throwing all four legs straight up in the air.

"I didn't see it," Merene wrote to Peaches. "But he did a backflip! A real backflip. No one-hundred-year-old man can do a backflip. I know you probably think I'm crazy, but I'm telling you, I know he did it."

She closed the letter with "Love you the most. Merene."

Her name was surrounded by excited hashmarks she had placed for dramatic effect.

# CHAPTER TWENTY-SEVEN

"How would you describe this place?" Peaches asked Jar Jar as they neared the end of a hike.

Jar Jar slowed his marching cadence. The fog from the mountains settled over the valleys, hanging in a vindictive haze. "Like a postcard for a wilderness resort. From hell."

"Welcome to Kunar Province, Afghanistan," Peaches said. "Your mountain resort from Hades."

One of the tree-lined fissures between the massive peaks had been dubbed "the Valley of Death." The wind in Missouri was like the gentle breath of a baby compared to the wind in this place. It intensified any condition. If it was hot, the wind made it scorching—Dante's inner-ring-of-hell scorching. When it was cold, the wind seemed to chill a person's innards. Out of habit on this cold day, Peaches ungloved his hands to make sure his fingers weren't icing up like his nose and eyes and lips were.

Jar Jar seemed to enjoy the cold. "It's like that saying, 'familiarity breeds contempt,' he said. "Unfamiliarity breeds whatever word is the opposite of contempt."

"Respect," Peaches said.

"That's fair. I respect the cold."

"I'd like to respect the beaches of The Gambia," Peaches said. "When I get hot, I can cool off quickly swimming."

"Hillbillies like swimming?"

"Yeah, man. Ponds and rivers are my thing back home."

"What about crocodiles?"

"In Missouri? Too cold. The worst we have to worry about are snapping turtles or bluegill fish that bite your toes when they lay their eggs. I lost a toe to a snapping turtle in a pond one time."

"Really?"

"Not really." Then Peaches returned to his previous train of thought. "When I get cold, it's hard to warm back up."

Peaches stopped suddenly, drawing a long, nasal breath. His nose twitched like a beagle's catching the scent of a cottontail. "Black locust." He fluttered his fingers and hissed.

Sure enough, fifty yards ahead, the rest of the platoon picked up on the scent of burning wood. It was a unique aroma, unlike the more familiar scents of burning pine or hickory.

"You're a bloodhound."

Suddenly Kenneth flashed into Peaches's mind. He had built a crude shanty long ago that served as a smokehouse for smoking hams and bacons with applewood and hickory and oak. Peaches could almost taste the meat, thinking about them.

Back to reality, Peaches gave the rugged landscape a once-over. He fixed his head in place, like a Little Leaguer tracking down a pop-fly baseball. "I think I'm more of a bird dog."

Jar Jar caught his gaze and saw a thin smoke trail dribbling out of the cavity of a mountain foothill in the distance. It could be nothing more than a shepherd child pausing to warm something. Or it could be an insurgent planting a homemade bomb. Or a local warlord sending a signal to narco-trafficking minions. After a pause and a flurry of glances through scopes, Peaches shook his head. "He's gone."

The soldiers carefully walked down a path inside a cave to inspect the fire's smoldering remains. Black locust wood burned slowly and threw a lot of heat like coal. It was a heavy, dense wood, from one of the few trees that could survive and flourish in the wispy-thin, rocky soils in the area. The stone walls of the enclosure were warm to the touch, though the fire had died down a long time ago.

Peaches squatted to examine a cluster of disheveled twigs that were used to kindle the now-dying pyre. Black locust trees had nasty, nasty thorns. They could shred a person. Daydreaming for a moment, he pushed a thorn too hard, poking a hole through his glove.

"An old man in my town says he's seen Christ's crown of thorns," Peaches said.

"For real?"

"For real. He's not one to lie either."

The black-locust log's charred remains failed to hide the human teeth among its ashes.

The soldiers tried hard to shed the invisible weight of being watched as they finished marching the remainder of their patrol.

Death was never distant in Kunar Province, Afghanistan.

# CHAPTER TWENTY-EIGHT

A few klicks down the road from the cavern, the platoon heard the steady, pulsating rhythms of a slim, nimble scout helicopter circling overhead. Then came the whistle of the oversized bottle rockets strapped to the flying machine's underside. Their swift dispatch sounded like searing meat, amplified. Then came the boom. Missiles hit the cavern hideout, ideally sealing it off from the outside forever.

It would be a reason to celebrate except for the fact that there were ten thousand other rat holes for the nefarious to hide in.

The voice of the military intelligence instructor at Fort Huachuca thundered in Peaches's head. "Think like the enemy. Keep your head on a swivel. Use the resources available to you."

After the platoon had returned to the base, a local village boy started watching Peaches. He found the tall, gaunt soldier odd. This particular soldier ran in circles around the outpost. The village boy brought his sister with him to watch. She was all he had left in this world.

After a few days, Peaches noticed his secret admirer, whose big brown eyes and curious face reminded him of a fox's. The children in Kunar Province were half-starved or half-beaten and sometimes both. The boy lingered around the GIs, hoping for any food scraps they could give him.

Peaches had heard the boy speak. But not the girl. She just watched and listened.

"These kids, Merene," Peaches wrote. "They're half-starving, half-naked, half-frozen. Send me what you can. There's only so much I can give them. The warlords steal anything worthwhile from them and beat them for getting too friendly with us. They sell the girls into marriages to pay debts. Some as young as ten go to live with men three times their age."

The boy decided the running man had kindness in his eyes. He whistled, catching Peaches's attention. The boy ran in place in a brief, frenzied bout and then stopped, pointing at Peaches. "Salaam aalaikum," the boy said, a hello in his native tongue of Pashto.

The literal translation of the greeting was "peace be upon you." Peaches really liked that. "Salaam aalaikum," he said.

"Tsengah yay?" the boy asked.

"How am I?" Peaches said in English. "I'm tired." Peaches leaned his head and cheek on top of his hands, feigning a snoring sleep.

The boy grinned. The little girl near him copied her brother. Their smiles warmed his heart in a way he hadn't felt in a very long time. The boy placed his hand over his heart as American schoolchildren did reciting the Pledge of Allegiance. He tapped his chest twice.

"Pat-man," he said.

Jar Jar had sauntered over slowly to witness the introduction. Another soldier, who was a Pashto interpreter, wasn't far behind.

"Did he say his name was Batman?" Peaches asked.

"P like Peaches," the interpreter said. "Patman."

The boy pointed at Peaches, raising his thick dark eyebrows and widening his bright brown eyes.

"He wants to know your name."

Monkey see, monkey do. Peaches patted his chest twice. "Peaches."

"Pee-chess," the boy said, faltering. He looked to the interpreter, asking what his name meant.

The interpreter responded and then pretended to bite his fist as if he were eating a peach.

The little girl found this amusing. She laughed loudly.

"Patman," Peaches said. "Tell him there is a famous superhero named Batman."

The boy nodded in excitement.

"Tell him I'll call him Batman. What is her name?"

The interpreter relayed the query in Pashto.

"Gabina," the newly pronounced Batman said.

"Ask him how old he is and how old she is."

Before the interpreter responded in Pashto, Batman flashed ten fingers and pointed at his sister. Then he flashed ten fingers again and added two fingers, making a peace sign, and then patted himself on the chest in the same manner he had introduced himself. She was ten years old, and he was twelve. The girl was small for her age.

Batman tapped his ear, turned toward his sister, and shook his head.

Peaches looked confused. "What? What does he mean?"

The interpreter rattled off the question. He, too, was interested. Then he said, "She's deaf. She doesn't speak either."

Batman looked upset and continued talking.

"He wants you to know that she is smart and can understand. She just can't hear or talk."

Peaches immediately loved this kid. He was the kind of big brother Peaches was himself. He thought about Brady for a moment. He would always be Brady's big brother.

# CHAPTER TWENTY-NINE

Peaches was giddy when he received his first letter from home sent by Barnabas. It was pleasant and polite, very much in the character of its author. "I've walked where you now walk," he wrote. "Alexander the Great conquered that country but couldn't keep it. It's a wild, fierce land, almost impervious to foreigners." This was an understatement.

Correspondence with Barnabas, whether written or spoken, was equal parts history, encouragement, and serenity. "The Aramaic language, which I've long studied, was written alongside Greek on a famous tablet in Kandahar some three hundred years before the birth of Christ. I've seen it myself. The way things were back then was similar to what you are living in today. Not much has changed." Peaches was comforted that Barnabas had seen the things he was seeing.

"You have an unseen protector. Of this, I'm sure."

Barnabas closed the letter with a quote from Ignatius Loyola: "'Go forth and set the world on fire. Act as if everything depended on you; trust as if everything depended on God. Love is shown more in deeds than in words.'"

"Are you reading a love letter?" Jar Jar asked. "You look really happy."

"The old man I told you about wrote me."

Jar Jar quickly changed his joking tone to one of reverence. He touched his fingertips together as if he were praying.

"That's the one," Peaches said.

Calmness and comfort were in short supply in a war zone with an unknown enemy. Peaches was grateful for the solace his elderly benefactor had delivered to him through the mail.

Jar Jar was comforted that his friend was comforted. He was calmer too.

# CHAPTER THIRTY

Merene, Kenneth, Sharyn, Barnabas, and Diz gathered to read the letters from Afghanistan each week.

"Send food, Merene. These kids are starving. They need protein. They eat nothing but scraps of bread for weeks on end—if they can get it. Send candy too," Peaches wrote.

Sharyn decided that the rest of Novinger needed to know about their favorite soldier. She made a poster with big laminated construction-paper letters spelling out "Letters Home." They hung it up in the Glastonbury Market and tacked to it the latest news Peaches had sent in. It was a little bit like the old days when newspapers would post a chapter at a time of books in the Sunday edition, keeping eager readers yearning for more as they looked forward to the next installment seven days later.

Pastor Sheila, who had known both Peaches and Merene since they were in diapers, made an announcement during the "Care & Concern" portion of the Sunday church service. Congregants shared praises and woes and gave updates on friends and family members in need of prayers and encouragement.

"It has come to my attention," she said, straightening her posture, "that little children in Afghanistan need our help." She went on to explain that the church would begin collecting shelf-stable foods, especially proteins, to send to Peaches for distribution to the needy.

There was no better uniter of hearts and minds than charity. Good people rallied around a good cause.

"There are people in need," Pastor Sheila said. "People that need love from Novinger, Missouri."

The food drive started out in fits and starts. A bag of beef jerky here, a few jars of peanut butter there. Cans of chicken and tuna stacked one upon the other in the church's fellowship hall slowly inched toward the ceiling.

# CHAPTER THIRTY-ONE

Jar Jar's eyes lit up when the troops received the first shipment from Novinger. "Peanut butter! I'll make you peanut butter chicken, and you will love it."

"Jarju, what's this called?" their sergeant asked later as they were seated to eat. "I want my wife to know how I died."

"Sir, it's called domoda. Gambian peanut stew."

"Day-um," a helicopter pilot from Arkansas said in his thick Southern accent. "It ain't bad, Sarge."

The stew had a tomato base thickened by unsweetened peanut butter and flavored with chili peppers, potatoes, and onions. Chunks of chicken sloshed in a big pot as Jar Jar ladled it out to serve over rice. He was so excited to see his fellow soldiers eat he couldn't sit down to eat himself, like a grandmother looking proudly over the family table at Thanksgiving.

"That's the best rice I've ever had," Peaches said with a wink.

The rice was plain white of the jasmine variety, grown in Missouri's southeasternmost region, affectionately nicknamed the bootheel. Peaches saved the plastic bag it came in. The brand's label featured "Grown in Missouri," which soothed him like a toddler's fondest blankie.

"Really, Peecher?" the sergeant asked. "Rice is rice, for God's sake. It's all the same."

"No, sir."

The sergeant paused his chewing, awaiting Peaches's reply.

"This rice was grown in Missouri."

"Oh, Jesus," the sergeant said, his voice dripping with sarcasm. "I can taste the difference now."

The table of fighting men laughed.

Jar Jar bought live chickens from villagers for the feast, paying several times over what they were worth to build goodwill and trust among the people. He and Peaches had lopped off the chickens' heads and dunked their bodies in boiling water after plucking the feathers from the carcasses. The birds were rangy and lean, unlike the plump, meaty chickens sold in American grocery stores. It was a lot of work but a welcome distraction from life in a war zone. Cooking's busy hands didn't leave much time for worry and anxiety.

Jar Jar was accustomed to eating in the same manner as the Afghans, using his right hand to scoop food from a dish with his fingers. He waited until his friends and commander ate before he ate. He insisted on cleaning up, despite repeated protests from Peaches. Peaches decided he would trot around the base for a while to burn off a few calories. As the sun began to set, Peaches saw a familiar face staring at him.

"Batman," he said, calling the boy's attention. He motioned for him to come to the entrance. "Jar Jar!" Peaches yelled. "Bring me some of the leftovers!"

When Jar Jar emerged from their kitchen, he saw the visitor. "Batman!" he shouted.

The boy smiled. He liked the cheerful Gambian. The interpreter emerged to speak with the boy. Batman wanted to know if the stew had pork.

"No," Jar Jar said. "I'm Muslim."

When the interpreter relayed the reply, Batman coughed, astonished. He clapped his hands.

Peaches and Jar Jar gave the boy enough food for a week. He carried it home, walking hilly miles while feeling its warmth. When he arrived, his sister looked up, amazed.

"God is great!" Batman said. She read his lips and smiled.

The children ate the stew using flatbread Peaches and Jar Jar had bought at the village market. With full bellies, brother and sister sat uncharacteristically warm in their drafty little hut. Neither child could remember the last time they had eaten so much meat. Holding each other, they fell asleep dreaming of peanut butter chicken and the Americans. A little dog watched over them.

# CHAPTER THIRTY-TWO

The soldiers called their base camp Little Round Top, named after a famous spot in the American Civil War's Battle of Gettysburg. Directly behind Little Round Top was a rocky cliff. Two watchtowers looked out over a small flat plateau nicknamed the Slaughter Pen. Again, a relic of a moniker from the Battle of Gettysburg. This Slaughter Pen was where a small scout helicopter landed and parked.

The soldiers' mission in their outpost was to monitor, track, and report. Shortly after the September 11th attacks, the United States had rolled into Afghanistan, carpet-bombing its capital, Kabul, into submission. The ruling regime, the Taliban, fled for the hills.

Top brass was very concerned insurgents would trickle back into the country to destabilize and destroy the new regime that had taken control. They were right. It was happening in Kunar, close to the Pakistan border.

The new government outlawed and destroyed the lucrative opium industry. Fields and fields of poppies were burned, crimping the global supply of heroine. Since their unseen enemies were so good at remaining unseen, poppy fields served as telltale signs of nearby bad actors. The soldiers mapped out poppies as they spotted them in their daily walks throughout the rugged terrain, trying their best to assure the locals they meant no harm.

There was a military saying that a person was "won" with heart and mind. Peaches and Jar Jar found this to be true. They were winning the hearts and minds of the locals with the food supplies sent from Missouri, and their distribution had become an almost weekly affair.

Batman, who had been orphaned, served as their distributor-in-chief. The hollow cheeks of the boy and his sister filled out a little in a few weeks' time as they ate consistently. Batman told the children who walked miles to get packets of jerky or bags of nuts that the Americans were not evildoers. He taught them the few English words he knew: "USA." "America." And his favorite, "Run, Peaches, run."

Peaches maintained his zealous regimen of running miles around the camp, which the kids found entertaining.

As the Americans delivered food, their adversaries delivered instruments of death. Weapons were flowing in from Pakistan to fight the Afghan government supported by the United States.

"He was right," Jar Jar said as his shovel hit something.

Batman had told Peaches about a cache hidden in a foxhole in a little valley several klicks down from their outpost. A boy with whom Batman shared food from Missouri said his older brother told him about it.

"Where did it come from?" Batman asked.

"The Ghosts," the boy said.

The previous foreign occupiers of Afghanistan, the Russians, referred to their mountain adversaries as Ghosts, a group of tribal vigilante guerrillas. They seemed to appear out of thin air. The rough terrain provided sanctuary for the lethal fighters who engaged in a brand of asymmetrical warfare that would have made the Viet Cong envious. The cache had AKs that were older than most of the enlisted men.

"Don't you find it odd," Peaches said, "that the insurgents have rifles older than us that are more reliable than our new stuff?"

The M-16 was deadly, but it didn't take much dust or sand to jam it up, rendering it about as useful as a caveman's club. The AKs seemed to fire better the dirtier they got. The M-16 was more accurate and sprayed bullets faster, but that didn't mean a thing if it couldn't shoot when needed.

Peaches and Jar Jar radioed for help. They would organize a sweep of the area for booby traps and IEDs left behind by whichever Bad

Santa had deposited those treasures. Their sergeant ventured from his command post to view the spoils.

"Made in China," the sergeant said, smoking a cigarette. "Sent with love through Pakistan."

Dozens of rocket-propelled grenade launchers had been dredged from beneath the earth. Dozens more AKs and ammunition clips were lined up next to them. The guns weren't factory fresh, but they were newer than what was probably being used in the cliffs and valleys at the moment. The contraband was arrayed by size and type. It looked like a death-themed garage sale.

How many pack mules had made trip after trip to bury and deposit the killing tools underground? The platoon knew more was hiding out there.

"It's the Fourth of July, boys," the sergeant said. "Light it up."

He called for the scout helicopter over the radio. They would feast on some of the spoils and destroy the rest.

"Day-eth from above," the country-bumpkin helicopter pilot called out over the radio.

The platoon stood far back from the cache, out of harm's way. Rockets leapt out from the slim helicopter, finding their target like pool-hall darts to a bullseye. The explosions from the munitions thundered across the valley, bouncing sound back and forth along the mountainous curtains.

Batman, miles away, heard it.

The Ghosts heard it as well.

The following week when Batman came around for food, Peaches asked him about the boy who had told Batman about the buried treasure.

"I haven't seen him in a while," Batman said to the interpreter.

Peaches tried very hard to channel his inner John Wayne or Clint Eastwood, remaining tough, cool, stoic.

Judging by the strained look on Peaches's face, Batman knew he wouldn't see the boy again.

# CHAPTER THIRTY-THREE

The following week, the sergeant called for a meeting of the local tribal elders. The gathering was called a shura.

Old men hobbled into a large room in the army outpost. Despite their advanced age, they sat cross-legged on the bare floor. Pain and hardship were ingrained upon the faces of the men, men who had not known peace in their lifetimes. The oldest of the bearded ensemble might have been in his fifties, which meant that man had survived the Soviets and the Taliban and a host of other warring factions. The United States, via the CIA, had armed many of them when they were young mujahideen fighters striking the Russians decades ago.

Amid a flurry of pleasantries and a gracious welcome, the sergeant cut to the chase. "We would like your permission to build a school."

The seated men liked what they heard.

The sergeant explained the details. The army would improve a roadway leading to a building that would be constructed by locals, with generous wages paid to the craftsmen by the United States government. "We want children, especially girls, to learn. All families that send their children to school will be paid."

The previous ruling radicals, the Taliban, who had been toppled a couple of years before, had outlawed the education of women and girls. The harsh reality was that most Afghan parents needed the labor of their children to survive. They couldn't afford to be without their work and the meager income tiny hands provided.

The sergeant made sure all of his troops expressed their thanks and gratitude to the old men who had come to the shura. They prepared a sumptuous traditional meal in honor of the assembly. The lamb and rice with raisins, carrots, and nuts were so tender and soft that even the broken-toothed old men could eat their fill. As ordered, Peaches had bought Afghan almonds at the market for the feast. They were a different variety than he was used to, softer and sweeter than any California almond he had eaten back home. He'd cracked their paper-thin shells in the palm of his hand as he'd walked back to the outpost the day before, snacking.

The group's leader, who wore oversized, square-framed glasses, stroked his long beard as he drank his tea. The soldiers filled an old-style samovar to brew a nonstop supply for their esteemed guests. Sunlight caught the glint of the whiskers upon his face, revealing a soft red undertone. He motioned for the attention of the interpreter. They traded verbal jabs back and forth in Pashto.

"He wants to try peanut butter chicken," the interpreter said. "It's halal, made by the American Muslim."

"Jarju," the sergeant barked. "Get this man what he asked for."

Unable to contain his excitement, Jar Jar responded with what sounded almost like a child's giggle. "Yes, sir!"

Jar Jar had been cooking batches of peanut butter chicken every week, a request from his fellow soldiers—and from Batman.

The old men dug in with their hands, pinching bits of meat in their fingers as they scooped up heaps of rice.

There were no leftovers.

# CHAPTER THIRTY-FOUR

Merene blinked and realized it had already been a year and a half since Peaches left for the army. He hadn't been able to come home on leave the whole time. Despite their distance apart, they had grown closer through a steady diet of letters.

She had been taking a few courses at the community college in Kirksville since her high school graduation. In addition to her work at the Glastonbury Market, Merene continued to learn about business from Barnabas. She knew he was wealthy, but the more she learned, the more she realized the vast scope of his business interests. The Glastonbury Company received payments and mining royalties from around the world. Barnabas maintained a handwritten ledger, logging expenses and receipts in excruciating detail.

"I probably should use a computer," he told Merene. "But a quill and paper hasn't failed me yet."

After she aced her exams to become certified as a paramedic, Merene began volunteering at an old folks' home in Kirksville to accrue service hours in preparation for a future career in healthcare. She found herself at the home on a Friday afternoon like any other. She checked on patients and carefully monitored their pulses and blood pressure readings. Some of the residents weren't verbal, locked in the dark abyss of dementia. Some of the old men begged her to take them for a ride or break them out of that place.

"At my age, I just want a girlfriend who can drive. That's my only requirement. She doesn't even need to know how to cook!" Irv, a retired farmer, joked. His wife had long since passed. He lived in guilt that he had survived her.

Merene found that her presence, her smile, and her listening were better medicine than any doctor-ordered prescription. The satisfaction she felt in caring for others was equal to the satisfaction felt by those she cared for.

A weak voice whispered from a room as Merene passed by. "Come," an old woman said.

Merene went to the bed, where she found a resident named Joan. She had never heard her speak before.

A feeding tube inserted the week before seemed not to be doing its job. The patient notes on a whiteboard indicated hospice care to keep Joan comfortable. The woman moved her hand to find Merene's, and the younger woman sat beside her. Arthritis had twisted Joan's bones into discolored hooks covered by blotchy, paper-thin skin. Merene clasped her other hand over the woman's hands to warm her cold fingers.

Joan had no family and no visitors. It appeared she had been an artist. Her room was decorated with several canvases of what looked to be her own work.

"I love your paintings, Ms. Joan," Merene said. "They make me feel like I'm standing right there in those landscapes instead of just looking at them."

Joan was listening and could understand her. After a few minutes of sitting on the bed, holding her hand, Merene decided to remain by her side. It felt right to do nothing more than to stay there with the elderly woman.

The woman's breathing slowed until it eventually stopped.

Merene stroked her thin hair and kissed her sallow cheek. A breeze fluttered the drapes of a half-opened window, revealing a screen to the outside.

"It's such a beautiful day, Joan."

It was hard to explain, but the presence of the old woman glided from her tired, weakened body, out the window. It rose upward into the sunshine of the day.

Merene was grateful that she had been there so that Joan didn't die alone. It was a dignified death.

She held her hand for a while longer, until the charge nurse came.

# CHAPTER THIRTY-FIVE

Merene found herself helping Kenneth on the farm over the weekend.

"You would love this, Kenneth," she said. She held a colorful, glossy flyer for a Caribbean cruise out of Galveston, Texas, in her hand. "It's one flat price per person. All the food is included, and it's all-you-can-eat."

The old man's eyebrows rose. He liked what he heard. "My girls would miss me, though."

"I'll take care of the cows while you're gone. For God's sake, you need to enjoy some time for yourself. You and Sharyn haven't taken a week-long vacation the whole time you've been married. You know she'd love sitting on the ship's deck, reading a good romance novel about men who take their wives on vacation!"

Kenneth cocked his head to the side as if he'd just been slapped in the face. He was giving the suggestion serious consideration. Farming was not just a line of work; it was a lifestyle. While it offered a wonderful self-sufficiency and independence, the work never ended. Merene's time at the old folks' home had taught her that the people who had regrets about their lives were not the most disappointed by the things they had done but by the experiences they hadn't had. Many had lamented not spending more time with their loved ones before it was too late.

"Don't tell me you don't have the money, either," Merene said. "You still have ninety-five cents of the first dollar you ever made."

"More like ninety-eight," Kenneth said. Farmers had to be thrifty and savings-minded. It was almost painful for Kenneth to spend money.

"You don't have to feel guilty about shopping, you know. You deserve something nice every once in a while. Sharyn deserves it too."

The wind blasted along the fence row Kenneth and Merene were out fixing in a pasture behind the house. Diz was nearby to keep curious, thrill-seeking cows from making a break through the exposed fence gap.

Though it wasn't Merene's intention to make him feel bad, Kenneth did. Sharyn deserves a nice vacation, he thought.

The brochure was almost too good to be true. Kenneth couldn't rent a hotel for as cheap as what some of the cruises offered. They had plenty of entertainment for cruisers at no additional cost. The young woman was right. It was a good deal.

"I'll consider it," Kenneth said. "On one condition."

Merene held her breath, listening.

"Do they have free soaps like the hotel we stayed in for Lover Boy's state cross-country meet?"

Merene looked down at her feet, shaking her head. "Of course they do!" Merene thought to herself, This was the deciding factor? The availability of complimentary toiletries?

Kenneth moved the tractor farther as they finished stretching a new section of three-strand barbed wire set upon a brand-new post. Diz helped eyeball the fenceposts into place, teetering his head to the side like a level until they stood just right. He barked when they met his expectations.

The cruise talk had distracted the work crew. Kenneth hadn't shifted the tractor safely into park. When he realized his error, it was too late. The tractor inched backward then sped up to a roll. Diz was distracted, paying close attention to the spirited discussion between Kenneth and Merene.

The dog didn't know what had happened when the tractor's huge wheel rolled over and crushed him. The big grooves of the tire then lifted his mangled body up and over again.

Kenneth saw it first, scrambling as fast as an eighty-something-year-old man with bad hips and knees could toward the runaway machinery.

"Oh my God!" Merene screamed. She covered her mouth with her hands, feeling the warmth from the panting of her shocked breathing. "Oh my God."

Diz didn't make a sound when he was killed. His body had been pressed grotesquely flat like pie-crust dough after a date with a rolling pin. His tongue bulged unnaturally out of his mouth, dripping a puddle of mottled, scarlet fluid.

Merene bent down on the ground and smoothed the fur of the little dog around his eyes, which were closed. Kenneth had secured the tractor into park and shut it off.

"Merene," he said, calmly.

She was sniffling and didn't look at him.

"Go get Barnabas. It will be all right."

Merene couldn't believe Kenneth. He didn't appear to be as upset as he should have been, having just witnessed the accidental death of the world's smartest dog. Maybe he was in shock.

She broke into a dead sprint toward Barnabas's house. As her lungs began to burn from running, her tears came all the more suddenly.

Barnabas had been reading alone with a cup of tea. Through the window, he saw the girl racing toward the house. Rising, he whispered a prayer and made the sign of the cross upon his forehead and chest. He met Merene outside the back porch. Out of breath, she nearly collapsed.

"Diz," she said. She couldn't say anything more. Her sobs wouldn't permit speech.

Barnabas looked down. "Merene."

She continued wailing.

"It will be all right." The old man took her hand. He began walking them toward the scene of the accident in the distance.

His grip was strong and steady. Though wracked by grief, she noticed the skin of his hands was thick and strong. She flashed back to the moment when Ms. Joan passed away. Her skin was crepey and delicate, like tissue paper. Barnabas's skin couldn't have been smoother or more supple. It struck her as odd, a momentary respite from her grief. He held her hand firmly to steady her gait as she battled tears and hyperventilation.

By the time they reached Kenneth, the sky had become cloudy and overcast. Merene's skin soon became covered in goose bumps as the temperature dropped quickly under the darkening sky.

Kenneth looked at Barnabas without saying a word. Barnabas's hands traced the nose and closed eyes of his lifeless dog. Blood wet his fingers. He rubbed them back and forth, dazed. Kenneth looked at Merene. She was still unnerved by his callous indifference to the tragedy. Kenneth walked to Merene. He put his arm around her, urging her to the house.

When Kenneth and Merene had distanced themselves from Barnabas and Diz but were still within earshot, Barnabas said, "Look away. You must not see."

Merene looked over her shoulder, startled. Barnabas bent prostrate on the ground like some sort of Buddhist monk. This crushed her. She wailed. He must be devastated, she thought.

Out of the corner of her waterlogged eye, she saw his arms raised in the air. He seemed to be holding a cup. A cup and a staff. It was an unusual posture, a bit like when a toddler tugged at the pant leg of a parent, begging to be picked up and held.

"Look away," Kenneth whispered.

"Dismas," Barnabas said. What followed was unintelligible.

Merene looked at her feet until the sun shone so brightly, she couldn't see them anymore. Kenneth squeezed her hand.

The next thing Merene remembered was taking a sip of iced tea that Sharyn had made for her at the house after she'd wiped tear-soaked hair from her eyes.

That and when Diz came bounding in the door Barnabas had opened.

Diz kissed her face with a lick and wagged his tail. He was very much alive.

# CHAPTER THIRTY-SIX

"Keep sending food," Peaches wrote. "There's always a need. We recently received orders to build a school. Girls weren't allowed to learn under the previous regime. The villagers are very excited, and so are we. Please start sending backpacks and school supplies. The kids will need everything. One last request. Send a winter coat for Batman and one for Gabina. He likes the Batman logo. We've shown him cartoons of his namesake. She likes princesses. They say we won't be here much longer after the school is finished."

Kenneth read the letter from Peaches out loud at church on Sunday. The congregation was excited for the children of the community whom they had never met. It reminded Barnabas of building Novinger's school years and years ago.

"There's nothing that brings people together like schools," he said. "Except maybe libraries."

The army would hire local laborers for the project. Men traveled for days on mules through mountains and valleys to be considered for the jobs. The wages would be the best for miles around. The army was careful in their review of the hired help, wanting to make sure their future contractors wouldn't prove to be insurgents who would work against them.

Peaches found the whole project fascinating. An army engineer was assigned to the site to make sure the roadway and building pad were leveled to appropriate specifications so that the drainage would be sufficient. The kids would have a nice open field behind the school to play soccer.

Villagers came from far and wide just to watch the progress each day. They knew Peaches as the running man. They had heard of the food he provided through Batman. They were very grateful for the young soldier and his friend, Jar Jar, the American who was a Muslim. The children, like his fellow soldiers, loved Jar Jar's peanut butter chicken.

For thousands of years, the Pashtun people had maintained an honor code they called the Pashtunwali. One of the tenets of the age-old code, preserved orally, was the showing of hospitality for visitors and defending them when necessary.

"Salaam," a man said, approaching Peaches. He placed his hand over his heart as he spoke.

"Hello," Peaches said.

The man giggled gleefully, pleased to hear Peaches's voice.

He gestured as if he were running and clapped his hands. Peaches's cross-country exploits were a spectacle for Pashtun people young and old, who clapped and laughed and cheered as he ran around the base and in secured areas.

"Run, Peaches, run," the man said. Batman had helped to make the phrase popular amongst the locals.

Peaches extended his right hand to the soldier. Their gazes caught.

In the man's face, Peaches sensed a certain familiarity that he couldn't quite place. It was like being reunited with an old friend, if, in fact, he had an old friend whose name he didn't know.

The man's eyes were definitely kind eyes. He chuckled as they shook hands, and his presence radiated a friendly warmth. Peaches felt like he was back home in Novinger for a moment.

"He speaks Pashto, but he's not from around here," the interpreter said. "I can't place his dialect. He's a friendly, though. He checked out."

Batman and Gabina milled around the jobsite, watching the men work. Thanks to the people of Novinger, they no longer had to beg for food. They had never been to school and couldn't wait for the new building to be completed.

The mystery man proved to be an outstanding carpenter. He set to work making all of the furniture for the new school: desks, tables, chairs, cabinets. He didn't like to use the battery-operated power tools the army had brought for the laborers, instead using handsaws as he tucked behind his ear the pencil he used to mark wood carefully before cutting.

"He's my friend," Batman told Peaches through the interpreter. "He stops by our house to make sure we're all right."

"Is he a relative?" the interpreter asked.

"No," Batman said. "Sometimes he stops by, and sometimes his little dog stops by."

"A Good Samaritan," Peaches said.

"Sah-marry-tan," Batman said, sounding out the strange word he'd heard for the first time.

"It's part of the Pashtunwali, to defend the weak," the interpreter said.

The carpenter watched the Americans talk about him. Little did Peaches know he understood everything they were saying.

# CHAPTER THIRTY-SEVEN

How could they be so cold? Merene thought. Just days after his accidental death and miraculous healing, Diz had gone missing, and no one seemed concerned.

"I can't believe you're not worried," she said to Sharyn as they sat together on a rainy afternoon, drinking hot dandelion tea sweetened with fresh honey.

"Listen, young 'un. There're some things we can't talk about or explain. He's been gone before, and he's always come right back." Sharyn reached across the table, looking straight into Merene's bright-green eyes. She placed her hands over the young woman's. "Always."

Merene couldn't decide whether she wanted to laugh, cry, or scream. She kept quiet.

Kenneth and Barnabas seemed equally unconcerned. The men ruminated about the weather and the crops in the field and how a good rain smelled before the raindrops even started to fall. Typical old-man chatter.

They both departed, leaving Merene and Sharyn alone once again.

"I need to tell Peaches what happened to Diz," Merene said. "He'll probably tell me to see a shrink."

Sharyn had a playful way of looking upward, her eyebrows arching as if they were stretching to touch the ceiling. She was hard to read. Merene didn't know if she was pondering some deep philosophical musing or thinking about what she would make for dinner. She said nothing, irritating Merene. But the silence, after its initial annoyance, was soothing.

They finished their tea. The bitterness of the dandelion root was mellowed subtly by the sweetness of the honey.

"Young 'un," Sharyn said again. "You do need to tell him. People who love each other don't keep secrets. You might find he has something to tell you too."

"What's that supposed to mean?"

Sharyn retreated into her upward glancing again. The silence returned.

# CHAPTER THIRTY-EIGHT

The sergeant gave Peaches, Jar Jar, and the interpreter special permission to visit Batman's house, if it could be called that. It lay a few miles of hard hiking into one of Kunar's numerous valleys. The whole time they traveled, the fighting men knew they were being watched by the unseen in the hills and rocky outposts. An army drone surveilled the men from above, carefully noting the location of the hovel they were approaching.

The sergeant hadn't warmed up to the unknown carpenter who had befriended Batman and Gabina. His story didn't add up. The man was a gifted craftsman and obviously not from the area. His best guess was that the man might have been aligned with the Iranians, who had an interest in exerting influence among the factions in Afghanistan friendly to the regime that had toppled the previous oppressors. Among warring tribes, the enemy of the enemy was a friend.

The dwelling was no better constructed than those in a homeless encampment one might find under a highway overpass near some big American city. Its mud bricks were drab and weatherworn. The front porch had a windowless lookout spot that had probably served as a makeshift pillbox bunker in the past. Mujahideen fighters had probably killed Russians by the score there decades ago. Their slain ghosts might still have lingered. It was dead quiet.

A small dog trotted around the corner, high-stepping like a dressage horse. It yapped and waited for the soldiers' attention to come its way.

It bobbed its head like those little desktop figurines given away at baseball games as it listened to the soldiers talk. It had a goatee at the bottom of its jaw and a large black spot on the top of its head.

"Look at that," the interpreter said. "Some designer lapdog in the middle of no-man's-land."

Peaches finally saw the dog. He stared, confused.

"Diz?" Peaches said. "No way."

"Who the hell is Diz?" the interpreter asked.

Jar Jar perked up, intrigued.

The dog barked a short, trilling reply and wagged its tail.

Behind him, the soldiers saw a pair of eyes looking cautiously at them. It was Batman's sister. When she saw it was safe to reveal herself, she stepped out into the open.

"It's just a damn dog," the interpreter said.

"Diz!" Peaches said.

The dog wagged its tail.

Gabina read the lips of the soldier.

"She can understand," Peaches said. "She just can't speak."

Gabina clapped.

Jar Jar placed a hand on Peaches's back. "Are you all right?"

Peaches bent down on one knee, click-clicking his tongue for the dog to come see him. He happily obliged.

"Diz," Peaches whispered, "dance."

On command, the dog hopped on two legs, pawing at the air, swaying back and forth.

"What a show-off!" Jar Jar said.

Gabina laughed. Her voice carried a sweetness and innocence only children had.

Batman came upon the gathering as the men were distracted by the dog's antics.

"Flip," Peaches said.

The dog quickly did a backflip in place. Gabina squealed.

"Diz," Peaches said.

The dog barked.

"You're a real dog whisperer," the interpreter said.

"Does the carpenter come to see you?" the interpreter asked Batman.

He nodded.

"What does the carpenter tell him?" Peaches asked.

Foreign languages sounded either fascinating or furious to those who did not understand them. It seemed like the boy's explanation had been drawn out for far too long for such a simple question.

"Oh God," the interpreter said.

Gabina was in full view, wearing a pretty yellow outfit they hadn't seen her wear before. The village children were so poor that they had few, if any, changes of clothes. It was common to recognize someone by what they wore.

"He says an old man bought her to marry."

Batman stroked his face as if he had a beard. He gestured as if he were using a hammer, then he stood straight, looking into the distance, as if he was measuring something in his mind. He looked exactly like the carpenter.

Peaches felt like his heart stopped beating. Jar Jar looked down and closed his eyes. Peaches knew he must have been praying for the little girl.

"This is some crazy shit, man," the interpreter said. "The carpenter comes at night to watch over them. When he's not here, the dog is."

Batman pressed his palms together, praying. He looked up at the sky and kissed his hands. "God is great," Batman said. That much Peaches and Jar Jar understood.

"He says he prayed to God that his sister would not be taken from him. That if she was taken, he would rather die. And…"

"And what?"

"The carpenter says he won't let it happen. That he came from far away to protect her."

"Jesus," Peaches said.

"No, no, no!" Batman shouted. "No Jesus. Sah-marry-tan."

Peaches was confused. "What?"

"Diz!" Batman yelled.

"The carpenter calls himself Diz," the interpreter said. "That's definitely not a Pashtun name."

Peaches couldn't believe what he heard. He didn't say a word as they hiked back to the base.

"What the hell's wrong, Peecher?" the sergeant barked.

"Nothing, sir."

They briefed the sergeant on the carpenter, who had promised Batman his sister wouldn't leave him for the man who bought her hand in marriage. It was within the realm of possibility that an elder from outside of the region might become involved with the two orphans, though the sergeant remained suspicious.

"Whoever he is, that son of a bitch can swing a hammer. I'd like to know where he learned to work wood like that. You should see the damned desks he built. They're works of art."

Peaches wanted to run to the school right that moment to see, but it was dusk. Too dangerous for travel. But he saw them the next day. The desks were made of olive wood, just like the famous gym floor in Novinger.

Peaches wasn't a bit surprised.

# CHAPTER THIRTY-NINE

"You'll think I'm crazy," Peaches wrote to Merene. "But Diz is here, and I'm sure it's him. You know that round black spot on the back of his head? The whiskered goatee that's perfectly manicured? I know you probably think I should get my head checked, but it's Diz. He knows I know too."

"I wonder if he does the flip?" Merene said as she read the letter out loud while sharing a tea with Sharyn. This cup was a spicy blend of wild ginger and ginseng, freshly harvested.

"He even does that flip on command. It's him," Peaches wrote. "Guaranteed."

He went on to explain how the carpenter came to visit the children and how the dog guarded Gabina. "He's never far from her," Peaches wrote. "He's like her guardian."

Merene looked pale and confused. Sharyn snorted then broke out into a hearty belly laugh. It took a while for her to catch her breath as she dabbed underneath her eyelids. Uncontrolled hysterics returned a time or two before she spoke.

"And you thought you were the crazy one!"

Merene couldn't help but laugh at the absurdity of the situation. It took her a couple of days to respond to Peaches's latest message.

"I'm not surprised," she wrote. "What if I told you I saw Diz killed in an accident? And what if I told you Barnabas brought him back to life? I'm not crazy."

She described the tractor accident, the walk back toward the house, the amazing, overwhelming bright light that temporarily blinded her. The cup and the staff Barnabas held up to the sky. "Diz trotted into the house like nothing happened. He even licked my face. He was fresh and clean and smelled really good."

"Did your girl break it off?" Jar Jar asked. "You've read that letter like fifty times."

"No, no. Just drama from back home."

"You sure you're all right?" The young man was genuinely kind-hearted and sincere. They had really become great friends.

Peaches changed into Uncle Sam-issued athletic shorts and laced up his running shoes.

"Run, Peaches, run," Jar Jar said.

He ran extra-hard that afternoon. When he finished, he looked up at the sky as he gasped for air.

He heard Barnabas's voice for a brief second. "Anything can happen if you let it," he said.

It seemed familiar. Peaches realized the quip was from a theatrical production of Mary Poppins that had visited his elementary school when he was a kid. It must have made an impression on his subconscious and stuck with him through the years.

After he cleaned up and went to bed, he was out cold as soon as his head hit the pillow.

Little did Peaches know tomorrow would be a long and painful day.

# CHAPTER FORTY

"Do as you're told," a creepy man with a hoarse voice moaned. Though it was in the black of the morning before dawn, he hid behind a pair of large patrol sunglasses. A scared boy listened. The man's stench was worse than garbage.

"This necklace will protect you from the blast," another man told him. "God's favor is upon you. Your brothers and sisters and mother and father will be rewarded for your bravery. God is great." He took a long draw on a cigarette. He blew its smoke into the trembling child's face.

"God is great," the boy said. Underneath his loose shirt, he wore a special vest the men had made for him.

"You don't stop walking until you're in the middle of the market. Get as close to the crowds as possible."

The creepy man said nothing.

The boy had hidden a Hershey's chocolate bar in his pocket. He hadn't told the men. "Save this for a special day," Patman had said when he gave it to him as a gift. "It's from our friends, the Americans."

The boy had never eaten chocolate. He had heard there was nothing sweeter in the entire world.

The men who made him wear the vest didn't like the Americans. He knew they would be upset if they saw the candy.

The morning was crisp and cold in the village, though the weather hadn't deterred packs of families from gathering for a bazaar. It was hard for the boy to walk with the vest underneath his clothes. It was heavy and hot. It rattled as he inched toward the marketplace.

He carefully peeled the chocolate bar's brown foil wrapper open.

"Her-shee," he said out loud. Patman had taught him its English name. "Her-shee."

The bar had melted a bit. He licked his fingers. There must be Her-shee in heaven, he thought. The sweetness of the chocolate made the blood rush to his lips and cheeks, warming his entire body. His tongue tingled as the cocoa flavor danced upon his taste buds. He folded the rest of the bar neatly back in the wrapper, saving the rest for later.

From a distance, the carpenter watched the boy through a rifle scope. He had spent the night on a rooftop in the village, waiting for the morning to come.

"'See that you do not despise one of these little ones. For I tell you that their angels in heaven always see the face of my Father in heaven,'" he said, repeating scripture.

He panned the horizon with his scope. "You make me sick," the carpenter said. "Show yourself."

The boy inched along the dusty street. He looked back for the men who'd sent him.

The carpenter found the man in the black sunglasses with his scope. The man's underling beside him held a black remote control. Even from a distance, the carpenter could smell the dark-spectacled man. He reeked of rotting flesh. The wind carried his ruinous scent.

The carpenter didn't have a clear shot at either of them. He tried anyway. The barrel of the carpenter's rifle whispered as a round hurtled through the chamber of a silencer.

The boy heard trilling beeps from under his vest. The boom would come in a few seconds now. The men had rehearsed the drill with him countless times. He could barely make his way through the bustling market.

The old man removed his sunglasses and gazed along the direction from where the shot had come. The man had no eyes. The sunglasses covered hollow, bare black sockets.

In his rifle sight, the carpenter watched as the man beckoned. He spit in the wind, disgusted.

The carpenter spit too. The feeling was mutual.

A brief ray of sunshine warmed the boy. He rubbed the charm the men had given him to protect him. He rubbed his fingers over the Hershee wrapper as it crunched and crackled.

It was the last sound he heard.

# CHAPTER FORTY-ONE

The radio traffic buzzed with activity at the American base camp. "Mass casualty event. Suicide bomber in a village market. Five miles away."

Peaches and Jar Jar were nervous. They had trained for a day like this.

The hatch on the helicopter opened. Ropes dangled below them, waiting for the clenched grip of their hands to lower them to the building below.

They slid down twenty feet of rope and jumped on top of a roof. The friction burned. They felt the heat through their gloves. A supply bag came flying overhead after they landed.

The wind slammed into the chests and faces of the combat medics as they raced to the scene of the devastation. The thunderclaps from a fleet of Black Hawks dispatched from who knew where pounded so hard that it helped to keep the hearts of the young men from leaping out of their chests.

"Keep your heads on a swivel, boys. Pay attention to your surroundings."

Peaches met the scene of the carnage well before Jar Jar. Jar Jar had paused as he radioed in the position of a dead man shot between the eyes that his companion had failed to notice.

Initialisms long ago committed to memory floated about in the heads of the young men. TCCC—Tactical Combat Casualty Care. The goal was to provide the fastest, most effective prehospital care possible. And, of course, save lives while doing so.

A bulbous transport helicopter was en route, carrying personnel and supplies to set up a makeshift operating room. The acrid village air swirled with dust, creating a noxious, choking aroma of burnt hair, seared human flesh, and fear. Men and women wailed as they found their loved ones maimed or killed.

"MARCH!" Peaches yelled.

"MARCH!" Jar Jar yelled back. It was an acronym for patient prioritization: major hemorrhaging first, then airway obstructions, respirations, circulation, and finally, head injuries and hypothermia. The most preventable cause of death at the scene of a catastrophic incident was hemorrhagic blood loss. Extremity bleeds became life-threatening in short order without proper attention.

Peaches and Jar Jar ripped through the medical bag thrown from their helicopter. Their first patient on the scene was a child clutched tightly by a mother. Peaches tapped the bright red cross patch on his shoulder. Then his hands flew around the child's arms like a spider weaving its web, wrapping gauze and compression bandaging over clothing in rapid succession. He grabbed the mother's hands and motioned for her to press on the tourniquet to hold it firm.

On to the next patient.

Jar Jar found a boy who was unconscious and straining to breathe. An older boy stood nearby, crying. Jar Jar bent down and propped the unconscious child's head up carefully. "Airway obstruction!" he yelled to Peaches. "Nasopharyngeal." Using his teeth, he tore the top off a clear cylinder of fluid then doused a clear plastic tube with it.

"Don't force it," Peaches said. "Slow and steady wins the race."

Jar Jar slid the lubricated tube in a nostril of the unresponsive patient. He maneuvered it down the back of the nasal cavity. He knew it was placed correctly when he saw some condensation from breath form in the tube. The child was breathing with much less effort.

"Yes!" Jar Jar screamed. He motioned for the other boy to hold the patient's head as he readied himself to move on.

Peaches ran to an alley, where he saw the back of a man wearing a clean white head wrap. The man looked like a piano virtuoso as his hands and fingers danced over the body of an injured villager. It was clear he knew what he was doing. The patient had an open chest wound that had been expertly triaged, likely preventing a cardiac arrest or worse. The man in the head wrap wiped a spot on the patient's exposed arm furiously. Peaches saw him draw a needle attached to a fluid bag, ready to insert an IV.

Peaches saw his face and was dumbstruck. It was the carpenter. He pointed in the direction of another patient in need of attention.

The soldiers lost track of time and space as they treated patients, stabilized them as best they could, and moved on to the next. The suicide bomb had been packed with nails and glass shards. Those who weren't immediately killed in its wake were concussed by a booming pulse or shredded as vile, minuscule fragments ripped and pulverized their skin.

"Drink," a soldier said to Peaches, offering a canteen an inch from his nose. Peaches was beyond parched.

"PAWS, PAWS, PAWS!" someone yelled. Another acronym, PAWS stood for pain management, antibiotics, wound treatment, and splinting.

A sea of armbands bearing the red cross now engulfed the scene. The makeshift hospital had been set up in a matter of minutes. Victims stable for transport would be flown away by helicopter soon.

Tired, confused, and exhausted, Peaches limped to the scout helicopter that would carry him back to the outpost. Out of the corner of his eye, he saw the carpenter seated on the ground. The man's robes were shredded and torn, crusty, and stained red and purple with dried blood. He rocked back and forth, tears streaming down his face. His lips moved, but he made no sound as he held a Hershey's wrapper in his hand.

# CHAPTER FORTY-TWO

An Associated Press photographer's bazooka-length camera clicked as a young US soldier stood with throngs of children, their teacher, and the gray-bearded tribal elders of the local shura. Mounds of school supplies were piled in front of the ensemble.

Papers, notebooks, rulers, pencils, scissors, books. The books were stacked as high as the tops of their future readers' heads. The article that would accompany the photograph noted that the supplies came in bulk as a gift from the people of Novinger, Missouri, to the new school in Kunar Province, Afghanistan.

The graybeards were pleased. Their children and grandchildren would have what they themselves never had: a safe place to unleash their minds for study.

"A famous soldier, Ignatius Loyola, said to 'go forth and set the world on fire,'" Private First-Class Jackson Peecher was quoted as saying in the article. "Serving the United States of America by serving the children of Afghanistan is the honor of a lifetime." The reporter who talked to him found the soldier to be more contemplative than his counterparts. It was clear from the attention the children gave PFC Peecher that he was their favorite.

In the corner of the photograph, nearly hidden by the others, squatted a small girl holding her little wire-haired dog.

# CHAPTER FORTY-THREE

"Well, I'll be…" Kenneth said.

Merene stared at him with an I-told-you-so glare.

"That's a lot of doggy paddling across a pond or two to get to Afghanistan."

Merene ordered extra copies of the article to frame. One would stay in the United Methodist Church and one in the Glastonbury Market. The others would be for her and Barnabas and Kenneth and Sharyn.

Barnabas read the article. He knew the joy Peaches was experiencing well. It brought back fond memories of building Novinger's school long ago. Merene pointed Diz out in the picture. True to form, Barnabas remained measured and calm. He seemed unconcerned about his furry friend.

"Diz will come back to us when he's ready," he said.

"So it is him!" Merene said.

"The truth will set you free," Barnabas said.

# CHAPTER FORTY-FOUR

The completion of the school was bittersweet for the platoon. After its first couple of months of operation, most of the soldiers would be reassigned to other posts. Peaches was both saddened and relieved. The laughter of the schoolchildren was the only relief he had experienced in that dangerous land since he'd been stationed there.

The carpenter had disappeared after Peaches saw him in the aftermath of the suicide bomber.

"Are you sure it was him?" Jar Jar asked. He hadn't seen him, but Peaches was absolutely convinced he was there.

With all the overhead surveillance by helicopter and the troops pouring in to set up the battlefield hospital, it wasn't likely that a man could have fled the scene of the devastation undetected.

But he had.

The carpenter finished the furniture work at the school and left. Like a ghost. The olive wood desks and chairs and tables were exquisite. The teacher of the school was hesitant to let his students use the fine new furniture. He eventually relented and found the children to be more conscientious and careful with their new learning place than anyone had imagined they could be.

"What do you want?" Peaches said to the dog, as if he could reply. He had classroom watch duty for the day.

Diz bumped his nose into Peaches's pant leg repeatedly to get his attention. When Peaches tried to bend down to pet him, the dog scampered off to the safety of the arms of Gabina.

Gabina would not only be the first girl in the new school but also the first girl with special needs to be educated. The teacher was surprised at how alert and engaging the young lady was.

Peaches waved to catch Batman's attention.

"Run, Peaches, run," Batman said.

The English vocabulary of the Afghan children was limited to "hello," "goodbye," and "American," but all the children enjoyed repeating "Run, Peaches, run." When night terrors of the dead and injured from the suicide blast preyed upon Peaches, it was by remembering the children chanting "Run, Peaches, run" that he could keep his sadness at bay.

"Have you seen the carpenter?" Peaches asked.

The interpreter repeated the question in Pashto to the boy, who was donning a new Batman backpack filled with matching Batman notebooks and pencils.

"He stays at night and leaves in the morning," Batman said. "The little dog stays with Gabina when I'm gone. He won't let them take her away."

The interpreter was confused and asked for an explanation.

"He says the man that bought her will come to get her soon, but the carpenter won't let it happen. He must be like a tribal elder or leader from a different region. It seems like the men in the local shura respect the carpenter."

"Where's he from?"

Batman seemed to understand the question, but he raised his hands in the air. He didn't know the answer.

"Talk to me, Diz," Peaches said to the little dog. "Tell me what's happening. I need your help."

# CHAPTER FORTY-FIVE

Diz was like Mary's little lamb from the nursery rhyme. Everywhere Gabina went, Diz was sure to follow. He stayed with her while she was in school with Batman. He walked home with them.

The soldiers patrolled the school daily.

Peaches was glad to see the school thrive. The good people of Novinger continued to send supplies.

Peaches received notice that he would be headed back to the United States to serve out the remainder of his enlistment in a month. His only unfinished business in Afghanistan was the assurance that Gabina wouldn't be taken by her elder suitor. Batman continued to reassure the soldiers that the carpenter, whom they hadn't seen in a long time, wouldn't let it happen.

* * *

Back home, Merene no longer blushed when Mrs. Peecher introduced her as her daughter-in-law. It was only a matter of time before Peaches came home and they got married. She didn't mind the surprising show of affection from a woman who was none too sentimental.

She pulled up to Peaches's house to take Mrs. Peecher to Kirksville to shop and get her hair cut, which would take a while, since a hairdresser was equal parts artist, confidant, and miracle worker.

The hard-driving guitar riffs of the Allman Brothers song "Whipping Post" filled the shop, where Mr. Peecher stood with his back to Merene. Wafts of cigarette smoke drifted up and over his shoulders. "We'll be back this afternoon," Merene said, almost shouting.

Merene had recently shared the good news that Peaches would be coming stateside soon. The announcement seemed to upset Mr. Peecher. Without even glancing at Merene, who looked chipper with her hair pulled back in a spunky ponytail, he muttered something she couldn't understand.

"What?" she asked.

"You'll be happy together," Mr. Peecher said.

She was a bit confused, not knowing whether he was talking about the trip to town with his wife or her and Peaches when he came home.

"I want you to tell him I'm proud of him," Mr. Peecher said.

Merene figured he might have gotten an early start on getting drunk for the day. It appeared he was already soaked, somber, and mired in unhappiness. "I'll tell him, Mr. Peecher. Do you need anything from town?"

Mr. Peecher shook his head with his back still turned.

"All right. You behave yourself while we're gone."

After the car had left and the clock had ticked thirty hashes, Mr. Peecher got to work. He'd spent a lot of time the last few weeks cleaning and organizing his shop. He did his best to inventory and catalog the contents of each drawer, toolbox, and shelf, making detailed notes in his best handwriting until the drink blurred the words and brought the work to a stop.

He taped a large tarp to the concrete floor with the care and precision of a seamstress. He set his easy chair in the middle. The Allman Brothers still sang "Whipping Post," which was on repeat.

He listened to it one more time. With his index and middle finger, he found the spot on the right side of his neck, looking like he was measuring his own pulse. He drew a pistol from his pocket.

Its bullet quickly and painlessly severed the circle of Willis inside his skull, ending his life.

Merene went to the shop to check on Mr. Peecher after dropping Mrs. Peecher off at the house. Mrs. Peecher was so impressed with her new haircut that she'd gone straight to the bathroom to see herself in the mirror. Merene was in a hurry, almost running late to work a shift at the Glastonbury Market.

She heard the same song as before playing again and found that odd. She saw the tarp and the easy chair in the middle of the shop. She ventured no farther, instead turning around to run to her car.

# CHAPTER FORTY-SIX

Two men approached the mud hut of Batman and Gabina. Batman had started a fire for the evening. It would be a cold, windy night. He didn't recognize the men. The taller man wore sunglasses, though it was no longer bright outside. Gabina had fallen asleep with the dog woven into her arms. His ears perked up.

"Boy," another man called, "come."

He didn't look familiar, but then again, he didn't look unfamiliar. A Soviet-era assault rifle was slung over his shoulder. The taller man stood in the distance, his nose in the air like a hound dog.

"You've been chosen," the man said. "Come with me."

"I can't leave my sister."

The fire he'd started had grown, spreading its warmth.

"She'll be fine, boy. When you do what I tell you, she'll be rewarded too."

The man told him he would deliver a special package to his school. "You'll be a hero," he said. "Your sister will be so proud. When you're finished, she can stay with you. She won't be taken away."

Batman wondered if the tall man in the distance was the one who had bought Gabina. Like a reptile, he had been inching cautiously closer.

The first man put his arm around Batman. He grew scared when he realized he wouldn't be able to run.

"Can I tell her goodnight?"

"Let her sleep. When she wakes up, you'll have made her dreams come true."

The tall man with the sunglasses disappeared from sight as the other man and Batman walked off into the darkness. Batman could see his breath. Air gusting down from the mountains nipped at his nose and hands. His ears throbbed.

As they traveled, the only sounds were those of the wind and their footsteps. The man's right arm readjusted the shoulder strap of his rifle intermittently. His pointer finger tap-tap-tapped the stock, a reminder to the boy not to consider running off.

Back at the hut, the tall man found the sleeping girl. "Dismas," he moaned. "Come out, you coward."

The dog perched in the shadows.

A charred log in the fire popped and hissed as it was eaten by the flames. It gave way as it collapsed to the bottom of the burning heap, sending embers scattershot. The shadow of a rifle's barrel moved against the wall as it scanned the room.

"Fine," the man moaned. "She dies because of you."

The dog watched the shadow crawl around the room until it rested in one place. He tensed his legs, taut like a coiled spring, and leapt.

Batman and his escort both heard a shot from a distance. They heard its echo again and again and again as the soundwaves ricocheted through the valley like a bouncing pinball.

"He found what he was looking for," the man said.

"What?" Batman asked.

"A trophy."

The tall man spoke to himself in the mud hut. "Fool," he moaned, admiring his harvest. "I wish I had eyes to watch you bleed and die."

He removed his sunglasses. Listening to the death would have to suffice. The little dog's breathing was faint but audible. Darkness filled the empty void behind the sunglasses. When the tall man no longer heard the dog's breath, he slithered out the door.

Embers swirled again as the fire was disturbed.

# CHAPTER FORTY-SEVEN

Two days, the soldiers thought. Two days. That's an eternity in a war zone.

Peaches watched as the children trickled into the school, sat, and waited patiently, ready to listen to their teacher. Yet again, there were two notable absences: Batman and Gabina.

"They hadn't missed a day up until yesterday," Jar Jar said.

After brushing his teeth that morning, Peaches couldn't rid his mouth of a sour taste. Worry was doing a number on his body, not to mention his mind.

"I know. Something's wrong," Peaches said.

"The dog hasn't been around either," Jar Jar said.

The soldiers were assigned to stay at the school until class was dismissed. Had the floors in the new building been carpeted, Peaches would have worn a rut into them from his constant pacing for the remainder of the day. Each minute that passed seemed like an hour.

Hang on, Batman and Gabina. We're coming, Peaches thought.

Peaches probably broke his old cross-country records racing back to the base as the kids departed from school in the afternoon. Jar Jar struggled to keep up from a distance.

Peaches spoke to the sergeant. "Sir, something's wrong." He explained about the missing students.

The sergeant gritted his teeth as he listened, accentuating a throbbing vein on the side of his close-cropped head. The vein looked like it was about ready to pop out from under his skin and explode at any minute.

The interpreter stood within earshot.

"I want you to monitor the radios tonight," the sergeant said.

"Yes, sir."

"When it's daylight tomorrow, you can go check on them."

Peaches blew a long breath of air from his cheeks, which had been full and rounded like Dizzy Gillespie's playing his trumpet. It would be a long night. There was no way Peaches would get any sleep.

# CHAPTER FORTY-EIGHT

Peaches and Jar Jar listened to radio chatter through the night.

"That's Lurch," the radio operator said. "We haven't heard from him in a while."

"Who is Lurch?" Jar Jar asked.

"He was a character on an old TV show called The Addams Family," Peaches said. "This family of monsters had a butler that was freakishly huge. He looked like Frankenstein's monster."

"You rang? Ughhhh." The radio operator moaned and groaned, mimicking the larger-than-life character's trademark response.

The voice on the radio moaned in some unknown tongue.

"I wish I knew what the hell Lurch was saying," the operator said. "I don't recognize the dialect. No one does."

Jar Jar had finally drifted off to sleep after the radio traffic became dead still in the wee hours of the morning. Peaches was reading a book Barnabas had sent him. He couldn't sleep.

A red light on the radio flickered, indicating traffic.

"Die," a moaning voice said in English. "Die, Joseph. Die."

"I guess old Lurch wants us dead," the radio operator said. "What an unfriendly bastard."

It wasn't uncommon for the Afghans to refer to the soldiers as GI Joes.

Even though he couldn't explain it with any semblance of logic or reason, Peaches felt certain the moaning man was talking about

Barnabas Hassan. He couldn't shake the image of the beloved old man from his thoughts.

What Peaches didn't know was that Barnabas had been listening too.

# CHAPTER FORTY-NINE

They outfitted Batman in a handsome green-and-gold waistcoat.

"Your sister has a new green dress," the man told him. "You'll see her soon."

"When?"

"After you deliver the package to the school." The man stomped his cigarette into dust on the floor of the cave they had spent the night in. The tall man hadn't joined them.

"You'll set the package in the classroom," the man said. "By the teacher. Then you'll walk out. You'll see your sister after school. Her new dress is lovely. She looks just like a princess."

The waistcoat Batman had been given was far too big. It dragged near his feet. He stubbed his toe and tripped on a rock near the entrance to the cave.

"Come along. Hurry!"

As he stood up to shake the dust from himself, he saw what had sent him stumbling. A charred, sooty jawbone, recognizable only by the teeth still attached to it, lay at his feet.

"Come on!"

He's a liar, Batman thought. He should know she would be at the school already.

# CHAPTER FIFTY

------

"Gentlemen, we're playing a game of keep-away," the sergeant said. "When the children arrive, you'll gather them and walk them out and away from the building. It's not safe for them to stay inside. We're anticipating trouble."

The school and the forward operating base would be monitored by drones above. The entire platoon was to remain on alert. The Americans anticipated imminent attacks from insurgents.

*   *   *

The man carried a package in a backpack. From where they stood, the school was barely visible in the distance. Batman watched him as he peered through his binoculars.

A row of mules stood hitched out front, waiting for their riders. The man smirked. The school was bursting at the seams.

As children arrived for the day, soldiers escorted them behind a bluff in a clearing beyond the schoolhouse. The teacher would give lessons outside today, he told his students. "Why?" they asked. Because the Americans said so. No one seemed too bothered by the request. It was a nice day to be outside.

Peaches stood in the front of the school, scanning the horizon.

Batman felt the dampness of the man's sweat as he slipped the slimy backpack onto him then tucked it under the too-large vest.

"Walk inside the school and deliver the package to the classroom. You'll see your sister soon."

The nudge forward he gave him was too strong for the boy. Batman winced as the backpack's straps cut into his shoulders, inflaming the spot on his neck where he had been prodded moments earlier.

Peaches saw a bright-green blob approach, moving slowly like a turtle toward the school. "We've got a visitor!" he yelled.

The lounging mules out front seemed uninterested, chewing casually and swatting flies with their tails.

Peaches put a finger to his ear as he listened to the headset.

"Step out of the building. Walk toward the boy, but don't get close."

"Peaches!" Batman shouted.

Peaches walked toward him.

"No farther," said the voice over the radio.

Peaches stopped and stood in place.

In his excitement, Batman stumbled and fell down onto his knees when he tried to quicken his pace. Breathing heavily, he rested for a moment. He had never been so happy to see someone as he was having seen Peaches in that moment. The pack tickled his back as its innards began to whiz and whir.

The man, watching from behind, was furious Batman had stopped his march to the schoolhouse. "Forward!" he screamed. "Move!"

"No!" Batman screamed back.

He dropped the backpack as he rubbed the bruises on his shoulders where the straps dug in. Next, he took off the oversized green waistcoat, soaked with sweat. Freed from his heavy burdens, he decided to run to his friend. Crouching down low like a sprinter on the starting blocks before a race, he looked ahead to Peaches, who stood frozen in place.

"Run, Peaches, run!" Batman said.

Peaches's last memory in Afghanistan was of Batman sprinting forward. The boy didn't make it to the finish line.

"Damn it!" the man screamed. "Damn it!" In an angry rage, he sprayed gunfire from his AK at the school building. He saw someone running to the valley in the distance out of the corner of his eye, too far away to pursue.

Though uninjured, the insurgent limped as if he had been shot as he made his way to the lair in the cave where he was to meet up with the tall man. He found the tall man waiting.

"Well?" the tall man groaned.

"It detonated too soon. Only the boy died."

"You worthless fool!" Breathing slowly and heavily, the tall man pointed his finger at the other man. "Get the body of the little girl and that little dog."

The man dragged his feet as he tarried across the hills and valleys back to the hovel where they had abducted Batman. The primitive dugout was as the men had left it, except the bodies of the girl and the little dog were nowhere to be found.

The man panicked as he saw the tall man trudging up the path to join him.

"Where are they?"

"I don't know, sir. The bodies are gone. Both of them."

The tall man motioned for his accomplice with his lean, bony hand. "Come here."

He grabbed the man by the throat when he came close enough. Turning his head, he asked the underling to read what was written on the wall. It looked like mud.

Choking, the man read the letters out loud, one at a time. "D-I-S-M-A-S."

"Dismas," the tall man moaned. He spat on the ground and removed his sunglasses.

The man in his grasp tried to scream but couldn't.

The tall man had no eyes. Instead, the black head of a cobra slithered out from inside his skull. It coiled around the tall man's neck and eventually perched on his shoulder.

The tall man released his grip on the man's throat, who stood paralyzed with fear. "Die," the tall man moaned.

The black cobra struck the other man in the face. He dropped in a heap to the ground and writhed.

The tall man watched until the other breathed his last.

"Dismas," the tall man groaned. "I'll find you."

# CHAPTER FIFTY-ONE

*Arimathea, Judea, Roman Empire. AD 33.*

Two men rode plodding donkeys into a small town somewhere between Jericho and Jerusalem to buy wineskins and food. The locals called the area Arimathea. The men's pockets bulged with stolen coin.

"They think they're better than me," Gestas said, admiring the horses hitched in front of an inn they rode past. The beasts snorted and stamped at the man, brash and cocky like the soldiers who owned them.

"Who?" Dismas asked.

"The Romans. But they're not."

"Not what?"

Gestas never replied. He hadn't planned to steal horses. An impulsive urge caught Gestas in the midst of an indignant fit.

"These are the ones!" Gestas shouted to Dismas, loud enough so the people on the street heard him clearly. "Untie them so we can take them to the stable."

Dismas trembled at the thought of stealing the horses in broad daylight.

"You're weak and disgusting," Gestas whispered to Dismas under his breath. "Have confidence, Dismas. Not even God can stop me."

The rippling muscle of a dazzling white horse twitched as Dismas stroked its shoulder, entranced. He untied it and followed behind Gestas, who led a brooding jet-black horse ahead.

They drew stares from the people they passed on the street, but no one stopped to question them. People probably assumed they had been hired to wash and board the horses. No one would be so foolish as to steal a Roman horse, which would almost guarantee a death sentence.

It was a quick job. The two men casually walked off with the animals while their owners lounged somewhere inside, hidden from view. They tied their donkeys in the spots where the horses had been. They carefully packed the food and drink they had purchased the honest way from a shopkeeper a few doors down—if, in fact, there was honesty in buying goods with stolen money.

Gestas brought his new black horse to a saunter as he rode past the inn, as if to taunt the unaware owners. "Come and get me, you bastards!"

Dismas followed closely behind, lacking Gestas's bravado.

Gestas's hand stung from the hard slap he gave the horse. It reared up and went to a full gallop in an instant. The white horse trailed closely behind. Dismas's long hair flew straight back as the horse tried to catch the black arrow Gestas rode in front of him. He felt like he was flying. The speed was intoxicating.

Safely outside of the town with no one in pursuit, one man lay drunken from the fruit of the vine, and the other lay drunken from adrenaline. The men lounged as they ate their lunch upon the grass on a lookout in the hills, gazing down upon a dusty highway.

"I can't believe it," Dismas said, still panting. "Roman horses!" He hadn't yet caught his breath, thrilled from the theft.

The alcohol imbibed by his companion began to speak. "I'll steal one thousand Roman horses," Gestas said, slurring. "They can't stop me."

Perched above the highway, the highwaymen waited.

"Well, look at this. A bitch and puppies. How darling!"

The exclamation startled the stolen horses and Dismas from their napping. Blinking wildly as he remembered where they were, Dismas looked in the direction the drunken Gestas pointed.

"There. A Jewish woman and children. Bring them to me."

"Why? They don't look like they have much. Let them be."

Gestas jumped to his feet like a circus acrobat. He towered over Dismas, who still lounged on the ground, wiping the sleep from his eyes. His thin fingers and sharp fingernails found their way to Dismas's collar.

Gestas inhaled slowly as he stretched his right hand behind himself. The slap upon Dismas's face startled the horses to snorting and trying to free themselves. Had Dismas been standing, he would have fallen from the blow. Blood began to fill the scarlet imprint of the hand left upon Dismas's face. Though it was the light of day, he saw stars twinkle above him.

"Do what I say," Gestas whispered through gritted teeth.

"Why?" Dismas asked again.

"Because I said so."

Gestas thought for a moment of biting the man's ear off but was distracted by the scurrying of his prey below. The woman saw the highwayman and gathered her children under her cloak as they began to run.

"You get the puppies," Gestas said, grabbing Dismas by his collar as he helped him up. "I'll get the bitch."

The black horse seemed to smell the coming hunt. He pawed and snorted as Gestas untied him and hopped atop his back. He walked it slowly and carefully, almost prancing down from the high ground.

The woman looked back, knowing she had nowhere to run. Still, she trudged forward with her children in tow.

Gestas, like a cat watching mice, licked his lips as they ran. "Scream," Gestas said. He closed his eyes, waiting to hear if his prayer was answered. Then the ropes of the reins burned his hands as he nearly rolled off his mount after flogging the horse into an abrupt gallop.

"Run along now!" the mother said. "I'll join you later."

The frightened children scampered ahead as they were told.

"Take everything, but leave them be!" the woman screamed as the black horse raced on by her.

Gestas felt like a gladiator in the Colosseum. He had a swift, fierce horse. He had power. He had a killer's instinct. The only thing lacking was legions of adoring fans watching.

Hoofbeats pounded the highway so hard and fast Gestas barely heard the child's neck snap as he battered him with a club.

He turned the horse on a dime. What a fine animal.

It spun effortlessly, creating a dust devil in its wake. The woman's vision was clouded. Her nose and mouth were overwhelmed as she coughed and spat.

Now, Gestas thought, I'm General Hannibal Barca high upon an elephant, ready to crush the enemy underfoot.

The standing child held the fallen one, clutching its bloodied face in its embrace. It used its body to shield the other from the oncoming demon.

"Damn you!" Dismas shouted, far outside of Gestas's hearing. "Let them be!"

Gestas's spastic jerking of the reins confused and angered the horse as it stomped and trampled and kicked. The bit cut its teeth and gums. It spewed a scarlet foam in a panicked frenzy.

The woman rushed toward the horse. The equine whirling dervish struck her before she made it, which, by then, was too late.

"Scream!" Gestas howled. "Beg!"

He wanted her alive.

"Dismas! Come!"

Still reeling from the blow to the head, Dismas heeded his master's call. He walked to the scene of the murders, lightheaded, temples throbbing. If he had proceeded any faster, he would have lost his balance and fallen.

"They're Jews," Dismas said.

"That means nothing to me. They're mice."

"Their leader, the Pharisee Joseph of Arimathea, will tell the Roman governor Pilate about this."

"Good! Let the Romans try to catch me. I'm a gladiator!"

He leaned into Dismas within an inch of his face. Gestas pressed on a blood-pocketed bruise in the shape of a finger under Dismas's eye with his own finger, fitting it into place like a puzzle piece.

Dismas's breath stuttered at the pressure.

"Jo-seph. Jooo-seph. Your Majesty! Come and get me!"

Gestas threw Dismas to the ground. He came eye to eye with the slain. Though the eyelids of the innocents were closed, Dismas felt a searing rebuke from their dead faces.

"I'm sorry," he whispered. He bundled the bodies closer to one another and laid them on the side of the highway. Their garments were stamped with manic, ruddy, blood-and-dust hoofprints.

"Get me my sword and a length of rope," Gestas barked.

"Why?"

"Because I told you so. You're weak, Dismas. You make me sick."

It was dusk when Dismas gained the courage to slip upon the white horse to flee. He had made it to the highway when he heard a demonic howl.

"You can run from me, Dismas, but you can't hide. Not even Joseph of Arimathea will save you."

Dismas brought the white horse to a gallop along the road, too afraid to look back at his tormentor. The drumming of the white horse's hooves drowned out the sound of its rider's sobs.

# CHAPTER FIFTY-TWO

Dismas slowed the white horse to a comfortable pace, assured he wasn't being followed. He shuddered to think what Gestas did in his absence. Guilt-ridden, he was determined to find Joseph of Arimathea, the Pharisee. Dismas wanted Joseph to know that while he was a thief, he wasn't a murderer, especially a murderer of women and children.

The Jew would report the crime to the Romans, no doubt explaining that the confessor rode a stolen Roman horse. Dismas didn't care. He recalled the time when he first encountered Joseph the Arimathean, though they had never met.

Gestas had kept an eye on Joseph, following him to an inn. He was known to be a wealthy man. He must have been very wealthy to afford all that he had given out to people in need.

Gestas seemed insulted by his charity. "Oh, how sweet. The kind man gives to the poor and destitute. I'm touched! It's a show, Dismas. He doesn't care about these people. It's nothing but self-gratification. That rich bastard thinks he's better than us. Take everything he's got when he leaves," Gestas told Dismas. "And kill him."

"Please," a tattered, dirty woman begged as Dismas made his way to the inn. "I'll take anything you can spare, sir."

Dismas paid the woman no mind.

The beggar woman went inside to the innkeeper. "Please. Let him sleep inside." She carried a listless, ragamuffin of a child on her shoulder. Sallow skin covered a skeletal body.

"Get out of here," the innkeeper said.

"Please!" she cried out. "He's very sick."

Joseph rose from a table where he sat alone. "Get her a room," Joseph said to the innkeeper. "Draw a warm bath. Bring clean clothes. Feed them whatever they want."

"As you wish, sir."

As he turned around, Joseph's hand caressed the child's cheek. "What's his name?"

Dismas drew himself closer to listen. The stench of ammonia from the urine-soaked child curled his upper lip. The woman didn't quite understand what was happening.

Joseph's gaze met Dismas's for a brief second. The kindness in Joseph's eyes struck him.

"Felix," the woman said.

"Felix," Joseph said. "Felix. A good Roman name."

The woman started shaking her head as the innkeeper came to show her to a room for the night. "I can't repay you, sir," she cried.

Joseph pulled a purse from his belt and gave her several coins, surprising even the innkeeper.

"Sir, I can't. I have nothing."

"You will. Someday, there'll be a woman with a child that needs your help. Someday, you'll help her. You'll do what you can, when you can. That's all that I ask. Is that fair?"

The gentle lowering of the woman's head sealed the deal as her eyes welled with tears.

Joseph stayed a while longer to see that his guests were attended to.

In the morning, Dismas learned the child, Felix, didn't live through the night.

He couldn't bring himself to rob the man, much less kill him.

# CHAPTER FIFTY-THREE

Joseph stood slightly hunched over, holding his hands in a knot behind his back as he listened. The man before him wasn't stark raving mad. He'd ridden in to see him on a shining white Roman horse that was most certainly stolen, matching the story from his confession.

Dismas was comforted by the tranquil presence of the Pharisee, who listened quietly as Dismas unburdened himself.

"Why did you come to me?" Joseph asked.

Pontius Pilate, the Roman governor of Judea, would not be merciful to the penitent man. But Joseph's gentle voice soothed Dismas like a cooling balm. The room the two men sat in was quiet except for the pale white noise of their own breathing.

"I'm a thief," Dismas said, unable to look his questioner in the eye. "But not a murderer. I wanted you to know that." Dismas dug into his shirt. He unfastened a purse filled with coin, which he extended to Joseph. "Here," Dismas said. "Do what you can, when you can."

Joseph left Dismas to himself in the room. Outside, he was met by a disheveled messenger who had run as fast as possible to find him.

"Two children and a woman were murdered by highwaymen," the messenger said. "The woman's body was hung upside down from a tree."

Joseph gave Dismas's purse to the messenger to arrange for the burial of the slaughtered.

# CHAPTER FIFTY-FOUR

The jailer barked at a manacled, bruised man who rambled on like the philosophers who overran taverns once their drink took hold. "Shut up, you fool!"

"Your mother's a whore," Gestas said. "You think you can kill me, but I'll never die."

The jailer banged a club against the bars. "You'll beg to be dead soon enough."

Gestas harassed the Romans who'd captured and beaten him within an inch of his life. He harangued them throughout the entire ordeal like a madman. "I'll never die," he said. "You think you can kill me, but I'll never die!"

Dismas hadn't said a word as he listened to his partner in crime from another cell. He clung to the words Joseph of Arimathea had spoken to him when he made his confession: "you did the right thing, young man."

Dismas traced his right palm with every finger of his left hand, as if by doing so he could divine the presence of the righteous man who had shaken it. Before they'd taken him away, Dismas had held the hand of Joseph, who cupped his other hand over his.

"Peace. Peace be with you," Joseph had said.

Dismas could feel the man's sincerity.

Their sentencing was quick. Gestas and Dismas would be nailed to a wooden cross the next day with a Nazarene teacher called Jesus. Jesus claimed he could forgive sin. Dismas didn't know if that was the truth or not. Honestly, he didn't care. He felt that Joseph had already freed and absolved him from the weight of his wrongdoing.

"I know you're there, Dismas," Gestas said, taunting him. "I know you're afraid. You disgust me."

The man's jeers drew no reply from Dismas, who, while chained to a wall in damp darkness, had accepted his fate with the calmness of a Stoic. His mind and heart were clear.

"When I'm free, I'll hunt you down…"

"We'll both be dead tomorrow," Dismas said.

Gestas's voice trailed off into the gentlest of whispers. "I'll kill you myself." Gestas rattled his fetters vigorously until the clanging came to an abrupt stop.

Dismas hung his head. "Peace. Peace be with you," he said.

Dismas repeated the line, like the words of a lullaby, and fell asleep.

————

# CHAPTER FIFTY-FIVE

Joseph's mind was troubled. He knew the teacher Jesus had committed no crime. The young man from Nazareth was set to die on a Roman cross next to thieves.

The Judean masses yearned to hear Jesus's simple stories, flocking in hordes wherever he spoke. It was the Jewish high priest Caiaphas who branded him a blasphemer. He must have felt threatened, Joseph reasoned.

"He claims to be the Son of God," Caiaphas said, "come to save our people. If we let him continue on with this talk, the people will believe him, and the Romans will destroy us for it. Better that he dies than our entire nation dies."

While Joseph voiced his disagreement with Caiaphas and the other Jewish leaders, it was no use. He knew Caiaphas envied Jesus, who had captured the attention of nearly everyone he came across as he taught. As a consolation, Caiaphas would allow Joseph to bury the condemned man in a proper tomb that Joseph owned. Jesus would soon pose no challenge to the high priest.

Joseph set out on his way to gather the belongings Jesus had left behind in an upper room where he had shared a last supper with his disciples before his arrest. He had been sold out by one of his own followers, Judas Iscariot, for a few silver coins.

Joseph found a simple pottery cup on a table in the upper room. He picked it up, glanced at it briefly, and set it down. He looked for other remnants of the rabbi who now sat beaten and jailed, awaiting his death. You're a traitor, Judas, Joseph thought. The man did nothing wrong. He spoke truth.

Joseph huffed and twisted his beard as he walked back to the gates of Jerusalem. He sighed as he remembered the clay cup he'd left on the table. He headed back to fetch it. The cup waited exactly where it had been left. He reached out to grasp it by the top with his fingertips. As he lifted it from the table, its contents splashed.

Funny, Joseph thought. It was empty before. He licked his fingers. The wine in the cup was marvelously sweet and light and pure. He drank it empty and set it down on the table again. Though it was late, Joseph would buy fine flaxen cloth to wrap the innocent man's body for burial.

He reached for the cup once more, this time by the stem. Filled to the brim, it spilled and splashed his fingers again. My mind is playing tricks on me, Joseph thought. A cup that refills itself! I must be drunk. He sipped from the cup, finding the fruit of the vine sweeter than before. When he finished, he held the cup upside down until it dripped no more.

Joseph cradled the cup near his heart with his right arm, as if it were a newborn, as he walked back to Jerusalem. When he retired for the evening, he placed the cup upside down on a table in his bedroom. Worry seeped from his mind into his body as he tossed and turned in bed. Early in the morning, he drifted to sleep. When the fingers of the light of dawn found his window, he arose.

"My God!"

The cup stood upright on the table, filled yet again. He drank from the cup until there was no more. He secured it under his tunic for safekeeping as he headed into the city. He prayed as he went, weeping for the man Jesus. From that day on, Joseph's body would no longer age.

# CHAPTER FIFTY-SIX

It was an unkindness, a group of ravens, waiting to feast upon the flesh of the condemned that unsettled Joseph such that he shuddered noticeably. When the barbarian festivities were over and the crowds had left, the three birds would feast upon the dying and the dead men nailed helplessly to the wooden beams below them. The guile and patience of the ravens unnerved the righteous man from Arimathea.

On the hill where the wooden crosses had been erected, Joseph watched Dismas as he drank the bitter wine and myrrh offered to him. A mocking sign above Jesus read "King of the Jews."

Gestas was nailed to his cross in the same manner as Jesus, to the left of the Nazarene.

"Jesus," Dismas said, looking at the rabbi, "remember me when you come into your kingdom."

Hearing Dismas, Gestas spat. It was then that Dismas saw Joseph in the crowd.

"Today," Jesus said. He had been scourged far worse than the thieves and had trouble breathing. "Today, you will join me in paradise."

Joseph heard the rabbi speak to Dismas. "Let it be so," Joseph said. "Let it be so."

Later, Joseph saw Caiaphas, the high priest. "You can save his body," Caiaphas said, "since the Messiah can't save himself."

The Pharisees gathered around Caiaphas laughed.

In the afternoon, Jesus, looking up to heaven, breathed his last. The sky above the hill of execution turned black. The light of day turned to darkness. Gathered spectators, like frightened sheep, scattered as the ground underneath their feet shook.

Gestas laughed as Dismas wailed for the dead man.

In the evening, a Roman soldier came to break the legs of Gestas and Dismas, still living, to speed up their deaths. Seeing Jesus already dead, he pierced his side with his spear. Blood and water flowed from the wound, startling the man. He ran away, afraid.

Dismas hung his head and cried until he slipped into unconsciousness. Then, in the darkness of night, Dismas heard a familiar voice utter his name.

"Dismas," Joseph said.

Dismas tried to respond. His lips were cracked and dried. His tongue had shriveled from dehydration. "Peace," he whispered. "Be with—"

Joseph looked over his shoulder. He was alone except for the company of the two thieves and the three ravens perched high, watching them.

He wrapped the body of Jesus in flaxen linens and laid it gently in a cart he'd brought. A Roman spear lay at the foot of the cross Jesus had been hanged upon.

"Peace." Dismas sighed. He lacked the strength to open his eyes.

Joseph took pity on the penitent thief. He hastily unwrapped the binding straps around Dismas's wrists and ankles. His parched body barely bled when the nails that had been driven into his feet and hands were pried loose. The cup of Jesus sat on the cart, waiting. Joseph had not let it leave his sight.

Joseph laid the listless Dismas to the right of the body of Jesus. Then Joseph reached for the cup, expecting it to be filled.

And it was so.

"Drink," Joseph said to Dismas.

The wine from the cup smoothed the rough, dry lips of the dying man.

Gestas moaned from the left-hand cross. Joseph approached the man.

"Joseph," Gestas murmured, "leave me."

Joseph placed his hand upon Gestas's pierced ankles.

"Leave me, Joseph. I hope you die. Die, Joseph, die. Die, Joseph, die. Die…" Gestas repeated himself again and again.

Joseph left and didn't look back.

The curious ravens hopscotched closer to the sole remaining condemned man once Joseph's cart had retreated from their sight. They had waited all day and most of the night for this moment. The largest of the scavengers sprang up to look at Gestas. While the raven rested on Gestas's shoulders, its head pivoted back and forth as if controlled by an unseen puppet master.

In delirium, Gestas cursed. "Die, Joseph, die."

The raven cackled as it bounced a diamond-shaped tail to steady its perch on top of Gestas's head. With two swift flits, the black bird's dagger beak found what it had been looking for. A glutton, the raven swallowed the man's eyes whole.

Gestas made no sound.

# CHAPTER FIFTY-SEVEN

---

"I was with him," Dismas said.

Startled, Joseph turned around to see Dismas sitting up, his legs stretched before him.

"It was magnificent. Indescribable."

"What was?" Joseph asked.

"I stood with the Messiah in paradise until he commanded me back. It's not yet my time to join him," Dismas said.

Joseph slowed the horse and cart as they approached the tomb, a large cavern scraped out of a hillside. He shook the dust from himself and turned around. He raised his head like a hound dog tracking. The sweet, subtle scent of lilies filled the place.

Now he took a good look at Dismas. Not a mark could be found upon his face. His cheeks were rosy and full, looking as if he had feasted and drunk for days.

Dismas climbed out of the cart on his own. He looked upon the body of Jesus. The two men lifted the linen-wrapped body and placed it in the tomb.

"Joseph," Dismas said. "Caiaphas will throw you in prison soon. But don't worry. I'll come to get you."

Dismas saw Joseph clutch at his chest with the cup held close to his body. "Keep that with you.  Don't let it leave your sight."

Dismas extended his hand. Joseph couldn't believe it. The puncture wounds from the nails were gone.

"Peace," Dismas said. "Peace be with you."

The two men stood together for what seemed like a long time until Dismas walked away, leaving Joseph behind.

# CHAPTER FIFTY-EIGHT

Gestas moaned in the darkness. A black snake climbed the length of the dying man on the cross, flitting its forked tongue.

"I will," Gestas said to the snake.

A hot, sharp gust of wind blew. The snake unraveled the ropes binding Gestas's wrists to the cross. Feeling returned to his fingers as they wriggled and writhed, shaking loose an agonized tension that had frozen them into place for hours. Gestas ripped his left wrist free, leaving the Roman nail in place with a chunk of his flesh remaining behind. He did the same with his right hand. The weight of his body pulled him into a forward fall, tearing flesh from his ankles.

Gestas, crumpled in a heap on the dry, dusty ground, couldn't see.

But he could feel. And smell. And hear. He had never felt more alive.

His shriveled fingers stroked the holes in his hands where the nails had been. "I will never die."

He sensed the dawn coming. He couldn't suppress an overwhelming urge to remain in the darkness. Standing, he pawed beneath his forehead, finding the open cavities that no longer held his eyes. The snake slithered and settled inside the hollow sockets.

The hot, sharp wind blew at his back. He staggered ahead to hide from the coming light.

Ravens gleaned the morsels of flesh and dried blood Gestas had left behind stuck to the nails still in the wood.

# CHAPTER FIFTY-NINE

"You," Caiaphas the high priest said, wagging his finger at Joseph. "I said you could take the body of Jesus. The bodies of the thieves crucified next to him are gone. The Romans want to know where they went."

Joseph said nothing.

"You," Caiaphas said, pressing his finger into Joseph's chest. "You disobeyed me."

Caiaphas had expended almost all the political capital with the Romans he could muster to have Jesus sentenced to death. The last thing the Romans wanted was another popular Jewish prisoner in their midst. Joseph was well-known and liked among the people. He wasn't stripped and beaten before he was placed in jail.

The clay cup stayed by his side. It filled once he set it down in the cell. Its contents satisfied Joseph's thirst and his hunger. Alone, he waited to be released, remembering what Dismas had told him. Minutes had a way of feeling like hours in solitary confinement. Joseph had no idea how much time passed.

Dismas walked into the jail. He found the jailer in a deep sleep, unbothered by the sound of his footsteps. Dismas clasped his hands together and whispered a thank-you as he raised his chin upward.

Joseph had been sleeping until a heavenly, floral aroma brought him to his senses. He knew it was Dismas. He recognized the same enchanting scent from when they had lain the body of Jesus in the tomb. Scents created powerful memories.

"Peace be with you," Joseph said.

"And also with you," Dismas said, his voice echoing.

Joseph brought his index finger to his lips to remind his liberator to be quiet. Dismas could hardly contain his excitement.

"It looks like you didn't even need me," Dismas whispered.

The cell was unlocked. The door made no sound as it swung open. The men slipped past the jailer, still out cold.

Joseph held the cup under his shirt. He also carried a length of the burial shroud that had touched Jesus. Dismas saw Joseph's fingers smooth the shroud as they headed outside to meet the dawn.

"He lives. His body is gone," Dismas said.

"What do you mean?"

"Jesus. The Nazarene. The Messiah."

The sweetness of the scent upon Dismas was too much to bear along with the thought of the crucified man yet living. Joseph's eyes welled with tears.

"I joined him in paradise," Dismas said. "He sent me back and has since appeared to his followers. They call themselves the fishers of men."

Joseph remembered Jesus telling Dismas he would see paradise as Gestas mocked them both.

"You and I will join him someday, but we have a lot of work to do until then," Dismas said.

Joseph saw two donkeys tethered outside the jail. Not another soul was in sight. "I expected white Roman horses," he said.

Dismas embraced Joseph. "Those days are behind me, my friend. Far behind me."

The men rode west from Jerusalem as the sun rose.

# CHAPTER SIXTY

"Barnabas!" a man dressed in white shouted. He motioned for Joseph to come closer.

The stranger greeted Joseph on the docks of a port on the Mediterranean as if they were old friends. He held Joseph's shoulders like a tailor sizing up a client to fit a custom garment.

"Barnabas. Barnabas Hassan. That's the name."

"Sir, I don't understand," Joseph said. "Who are you?"

"You're Barnabas Hassan. What's not to understand?"

Before Joseph could reply, the man shouted, startling him. "Dismas! I haven't forgotten you!"

Joseph turned around to find his traveling companion gone.

A dog barked.

"Dismas!" the man said. "Come along! You know we've got a schedule to keep!"

A wiry-haired little dog sprung aboard the deck of a boat the man in white was in the process of unmooring. He had already unloaded the packs from the donkeys that had carried the men to the sea's shore.

"Sir, I don't understand," Joseph said again.

"What's not to understand? You're a brand-new man, Barnabas Hassan. If it weren't for old Caiaphas and those pesky Romans, you probably could have kept your name. It's best to keep them guessing."

The little dog barked.

"Man's best friend indeed. He'll not leave your side. We've got very important plans for you, Barnabas Hassan."

The dog barked again.

"You, too, Dismas. You too."

The dog wagged his tail.

"I've mapped everything out for you." He handed Joseph a collection of scrolls.

"Dismas?" Joseph asked.

"It is he!" the man said, looking at the dog. "Sometimes he'll walk on four legs, and other times he'll walk on two. That's for the master to decide. You'll both set sail for Glastonbury."

"Where's Glastonbury?"

"Far beyond the Romans, for the time being, at least. Don't let the weather fool you; it's really rather lovely there. A bit rainy, but the sun shines brightest after a storm, anyway." The man picked up a staff and handed it to Joseph. "When you find the spot I've marked, you'll set this staff into the ground. A flowering hawthorn will appear."

"No, really!" the man said as he saw Joseph's eyes widen. "You'll have to trust me. There's really only one way to find out!" The man raised his hand to the sky over the sea. "Let this guide you." No sooner had he finished speaking than a magnificent rainbow appeared. "Safe travels, Barnabas Hassan. Peace be with you."

The dog barked.

"Peace be with you, Dismas."

"And also with you," Barnabas Hassan said.

When he lowered his gaze from the sky, the stranger in white had disappeared.

# CHAPTER SIXTY-ONE

Barnabas Hassan and his faithful four-legged companion, Dismas, set sail for Glastonbury.

The cup sustained them during the voyage. A net the stranger packed for them caught fish the very second Barnabas Hassan tossed it into the waters. They awoke in the mornings to find bread waiting for them. They followed the rainbow until they found its end.

Sloshing on foot from the coast into the moors, Dismas ran ahead. The dog had read the map a thousand times during their time at sea. The bottoms of his furry white legs were stained green from the soggy grass in the marshy land. Dismas barked in the distance as Barnabas followed behind.

"I'm coming. I'm coming."

Dismas, though a terrier, pinned his ears and nose forward like a pointer to the spot they were looking for on a hillside.

"Glastonbury it is," Barnabas said.

The land was lush and green. The staff he carried was slick from the misty air and from the rain the dark clouds above brought upon them that day.

As they approached the spot marked for them, Dismas bowed his head. Barnabas did the same. The staff crackled and sparked as Barnabas held it in the air for a moment, preparing to strike the earth. Its energy coursed through Barnabas's entire body. When the staff hit the soil, the storm clouds immediately disappeared. The pair blinked and rubbed their eyes as they adjusted to an immediate, overwhelming sunshine. When their eyes were fit to see, a huge hawthorn tree stood before them, its canopy shading them from the intense light surrounding them.

Over the hills and meadows in the distance stood an outcropping of rock, a tor. Barnabas and Dismas saw flames burning brightly in the sky above the tor. When the flames disappeared, the great hawthorn, its leafy green branches bearing sharp thorns, instantly burst with shining white flowers right before them. Man and dog savored the dazzling, perfumed scent of heaven the blooms carried.

Years later, they stood at the hawthorn again as they prepared to leave Glastonbury. Long before that time, Barnabas Hassan and Dismas the dog had realized they hadn't aged a day.

Barnabas Hassan traveled lightly, carrying only the staff, the cup, and the burial shroud, with his faithful four-legged companion by his side.

# CHAPTER SIXTY-TWO

---

*Walter Reed Army Medical Center-Bethesda, Maryland*

Peaches opened his eyes for the first time in weeks. The first thing he saw was Merene's face. He blinked. When he opened his eyes again, she was still there. He raised his hands to see an IV drip attached to his arm alongside what seemed like a dozen different tubes and monitors.

"Good morning, handsome." Merene rose from her chair and kissed Peaches's cheek. "You're going home soon."

Peaches's head and neck were in some sort of helmet and brace that looked and felt like a medieval torture device. While he couldn't see Barnabas, he knew he was in the room too.

"You set the world on fire," Barnabas said, "and it almost burned you up with it."

Peaches closed his eyes and exhaled, relieved. It was good to see Merene and to hear Barnabas's voice.

"What happened?" Peaches asked.

An army doctor entered the room for morning rounds. "Glad to see you awake, soldier."

"Yes, sir."

"I see you're a combat medic."

"Yes, sir."

"Good. We can speak the same language."

"Yes, sir."

"Doctor, what happened?" Merene asked.

The doctor scanned some pages in a clipboard he carried. "The enemy strapped an explosive to some poor kid. They intended to level the school you helped build in Kunar."

"Batman," Peaches said.

"What?" the doctor asked.

"I'm sorry, sir. The boy's name was Patman. We nicknamed him Batman."

The doctor looked annoyed. "They have no respect for human life. Who the hell kills schoolchildren?"

It was then Peaches realized Batman hadn't made it.

"The extreme and sudden change in air pressure from the vacuum and then the explosion from the blast caused severe barotrauma."

"Pneumothorax?" Merene asked.

"Yes, ma'am. That's the diagnosis."

A balloon down the hall popped.

"How's that for timing?" the doctor said. "Your lungs filled with air so fast that they ruptured and collapsed like that balloon that just popped. You were lucky, soldier. One of the locals carried you far enough from the point of the detonation that it allowed you to be here now. Without him, you'd be dead." The doctor looked down at his clipboard. "It says here your partner Jarju saw him. He didn't know his name but says that you referred to him as 'the carpenter.'"

"Sir," Peaches said. He took as deep a breath as his weakened state allowed. "Did the carpenter live?"

"I don't know, but let's hope so. We need as many of the good guys over there as we can get."

"Sir, what about the school?"

"You're a hero, young man. No one else was injured. The school sustained minor damage, but it's still standing. You made headlines around the world."

The doctor reviewed the rest of his medical history along with Merene. Peaches had broken vertebrae in his neck and had been in an induced coma to make sure swelling didn't damage his spinal cord or brain.

"Here's the bad news, young man. Uncle Sam is medically discharging you from the army. I want you to go home and study hard." He turned to look at Merene. "You'll both make fine doctors someday."

"Yes, sir."

"Thank you, Doctor," Merene said. "I mean, sir."

The doctor turned to Barnabas. He couldn't figure out if the man was his father or grandfather. "Sir, do you have any questions?"

"The man that saved our soldier—do we know where he is?"

"No, but there weren't any reported civilian casualties except for the boy."

Barnabas clasped his hands together as if he were praying and bowed slightly.

The doctor left the room.

"I'm going down the hall for a moment," Barnabas said. "I'll leave you two alone."

Peaches yawned, which hurt.

"Close your eyes," Merene said. "But listen. Your dad… your dad's gone. Kenneth and Sharyn are back home, taking care of your mom."

Peaches opened his eyes as Merene told him about how she had heard the Allman Brothers song playing when she left him and then again when she found his body.

"You know," Peaches said, "this is terrible, but I'm actually relieved."

Merene squeezed his hand. She had managed to maintain her composure until that point. "I felt that way with my mom," she said, sniffling. "I'll always miss her, but at least her pain is gone."

"Did Diz come home?"

"Not yet. Barnabas doesn't seem to be too worried, though. He told me it's mind over matter. If he doesn't mind, it doesn't matter."

Peaches tried to laugh but winced instead.

Merene kissed Peaches on the forehead, and he soon fell asleep.

# CHAPTER SIXTY-THREE

Peaches was released from Walter Reed Medical Center a week later. Barnabas and Merene drove the whole way back to Missouri, where they would bury Mr. Peecher once they arrived.

Days later, looking down at the fresh dirt covering his father's grave, Peaches noticed a ray of sunlight shining on Brady's headstone right next to it.

"Come home, Diz," Peaches whispered. "I need you."

Barnabas heard him. He placed his arm around Peaches. "You'll see them again, young man; I promise you. Dismas will return. I know he's out there somewhere."

Barnabas saw a soldier in uniform walking across the cemetery. "You've got a visitor."

Peaches wiped his eyes with his shirtsleeve. Then he felt a hand on his back. When he turned around, Jar Jar was staring him in the face.

"I'm so sorry, Peaches."

They hugged.

"How'd you get here?"

"Your neighbor pulled some strings, I think."

Barnabas tipped his porkpie hat to the pair.

Jar Jar bent almost into a ninety-degree angle as he bowed to Merene when she walked over to the reunited soldiers. "Jarju," he said, extending his hand. "Pleased to meet you, ma'am."

"He'll be my best man when we get married," Peaches said.

Merene blushed as Sharyn hooted her trademark laugh.

"Young 'un," Sharyn said, "I think I've heard it all now. A marriage proposal at a funeral?"

"Jarju, do you have a first name?" Kenneth asked.

"That's a good question!" Peaches said. He didn't remember Jarju's first name at the moment.

"Alagie. But please call me Jar Jar. I'm used to it."

"Al," Kenneth said. "I'll call you Al because I'll remember that."

"You can call me Al, then," Jar Jar said.

Merene and Jar Jar placed their arms on each side of Peaches as they helped him back from the cemetery to a lunch waiting at the church.

# CHAPTER SIXTY-FOUR

Jar Jar knew what movie stars felt like as he tried to make his way to sit down in the fellowship hall of Novinger United Methodist Church, where a lunch was served after the graveside service for Peaches's father.

"So nice to meet you."

"Thank you for your service, young man."

"God bless you."

"My, you're handsome. I've got a granddaughter you should meet!"

Little old ladies lined up to hug him. The men preferred to shake his hand and offer a friendly slap on the back. One grandmother was so bold as to pinch his cheeks before planting a little peck on them.

Another started crying, which nearly caused a chain reaction amongst the congregants. "I'm just so proud of you boys," the woman said, looking over at Peaches, who was seated. "Jesus said to love the little children, and that's exactly what you did when you built that school over there."

Jar Jar beamed with pride when he saw an entire wall of the fellowship hall dedicated to chronicling their work in Afghanistan. It was plastered with articles and pictures from the school building project, along with charts and graphs of all of the supplies sent by the People in Need program. He had to look away when he saw a picture of Batman holding a Hershey's chocolate bar. Peaches had to look away too.

The church ladies brought a platter of sandwiches to the table where Peaches, Mrs. Peecher, Merene, Kenneth, Sharyn, and Jar Jar sat. Sharyn had caught Jar Jar admiring a stand of hibiscus flowers outside of the fellowship hall before he stepped inside.

"Do you like my hibiscuses?"

"I love them," he said, in between sandwich bites. "I'll make you a sweet drink if you can spare me a few blooms. We call it wonjo in The Gambia. It's very refreshing. You'll like it."

"I'd like to try it," Sharyn said.

Kenneth spoke up. "Al, I've known your buddy since he was an even skinnier puppy than he is now, and he's never even made me so much as a glass of tea!"

"I'll make you peanut butter chicken to go with it," Jar Jar said.

"Al, you just get better and better!"

"You'll like it," Peaches said. "I promise you."

Kenneth slapped his belly proudly like a department-store Santa Claus. "There's not much I don't like!"

Jar Jar got up and made his way over to the dessert table, which featured a menagerie of home-baked cakes, pies, and cookies. He felt like every eye in the gathering was on him as he made his selection. He looked back at Peaches.

"Listen," Peaches said. "Just take a little bit of everything. Otherwise, they'll force-feed you into trying them all anyway."

The old folks clapped when they saw his paper plate loaded with a hearty sampling of the offerings.

Merene got up to help bus tables with Mrs. Peecher. Kenneth and Sharyn followed suit. Barnabas sat down next to Peaches.

"Barnabas Hassan," he said, extending his hand to Jar Jar.

Jar Jar bowed reflexively. This was the holy man Peaches had told him so much about. Barnabas clasped the soldier's hand with both of his.

"Peace be with you," Barnabas said.

"And with you," Jar Jar said.

"Please be seated, young man."

Jar Jar's ears tingled curiously from the soothing sound of Barnabas's voice. He felt his cheeks blush.

"We want to hear about the blast," Peaches said. "I slept through it, and my memory is a bit fuzzy."

Jar Jar looked over to Barnabas and bowed his head in respect. Barnabas bowed his head in return. Jar Jar began.

"The carpenter came to the school before anyone had arrived. Not even the teacher was there."

"How'd you know that?" Peaches asked.

"He left a note with instructions."

"I'm surprised he could read and write."

Barnabas listened. Jar Jar continued.

"He made it clear the children were to be brought behind the school but that otherwise it should look like any other day. He must have known an attack was coming. I didn't see him until Batman started walking toward the school with the backpack. You didn't see him either."

"No, I didn't. I remember Batman putting the backpack down and running, and that's about it. I didn't even hear the explosion."

"I don't know where the carpenter came from. No one could figure it out. I think he dug a hole waiting. We had drones watching, and they saw nothing up until that point. He was wounded. Badly. He came running to you and threw you out of the way. This was all seconds or less before the blast. I saw him holding his side as he ran. When he went to grab you, his right hand was stained bright red with his own blood. And you know about how we always joked about his perfume?"

"Of course," Peaches said. "He always smelled like flowers. Like lilies."

"His handprint on your uniform smelled exactly like his perfume, even after the dust and debris from the blast covered you. Somebody sprayed rounds at the school right when the blast hit."

"I'm sure it was the trigger man," Peaches said.

"Yes. The drones found the guy hiding in the hills after he shot, but nobody could take him out during all the chaos after the bomb went off. He was definitely trying to kill the carpenter."

"Or me," Peaches said.

"No. If he wanted you dead, he could have shot you before the detonation. I think he needed you to bait the carpenter out from hiding. Here's where it gets crazy, though. The blood trail from where the carpenter was to right where he lifted you away from the blast was there on the ground, easy to follow. But we found no sign of his body. He survived and ran off, which is why I think the trigger man was shooting at him. There was no more blood, though, which doesn't make sense. I for sure saw his hand soaked. He had been wounded pretty badly before that point."

Jar Jar paused and looked up at the ceiling.

"So I think, okay, he's going to hide out somewhere for a while. The first place I think of is Batman's place. After we secure the school site, I ask for permission to go to where Batman lived. It's broad daylight, and we have drones and helicopters buzzing all over the place. We get there, and that wedding dress Gabina was wearing has blood on it and a bullet hole in it. It's inside out, bunched up, and thrown on the dirt floor. There were some bloody dog tracks that stopped by where her body must have been, but the dog's body is nowhere to be found. I go looking around, and I see the empty hanger that had held that princess dress we gave her."

"She loved that dress," Peaches said. His voice cracked.

"I know she did," Jar Jar said, looking down. He continued. "Where the dog's footprints had ended, they were replaced by a man's footprints. No spot where the dog lay down to die or anything, no break in the footprints other than that they changed their size and shape. It's really weird. But the smell! It smelled like flowers everywhere! I know the carpenter had to have been there. You know that scent, man. It's distinctive. Something you remember clearly."

Peaches shrugged. "I couldn't forget it if I tried."

Jar Jar looked over at Barnabas. "I know you must think I'm crazy, sir, but this scent was like pure beauty. Like I can't even describe it with words. Strong too. Overpowering."

"Like heaven," Barnabas said.

Jar Jar smiled. "Yes, sir! Like if heaven had a scent! The trail of man footprints led to a fresh grave. I think the carpenter buried Gabina in the princess dress with the dog."

Jar Jar looked over at Barnabas again to explain. "This little dog came around one day out of nowhere and stayed with this little girl. Then we found out the carpenter had stayed with these kids too. They were like some sort of guardian angels."

Barnabas looked like he could cry at any minute. Peaches caught him looking over at the wall with the pictures from Afghanistan.

"It gets better," Jar Jar said. "We found the body of an insurgent not far from the grave. He had puncture wounds on his neck like Dracula had struck him. I took pictures of the body. Drone footage matched it up, and it was the trigger man that detonated the bomb at the school."

"An eye for an eye," Peaches said.

Jar Jar took a breath. "Get this: he was killed by a snake bite."

"I mean, that's not so out of the ordinary. There are vipers all over Afghanistan," Peaches said.

"I know," Jar Jar said. "Especially the ones that walk on two feet."

"That's no lie," Peaches whispered.

"Sarge wanted pictures of everything. The body too. We bagged it and brought it back. The hospital got a positive identification from pictures of the wound and confirmed it with some kind of lab sample. One of the doctors had toured in Iraq and had done research on snake bites and antivenom. Apparently, there's no universal antivenom—treating snakebite correctly depends on knowing the specific snake species that bit. The snake that killed that guy wasn't from Afghanistan. Not even close."

"What was it?" Peaches asked.

"A black desert cobra. Native to Israel and the Middle East." Jar Jar took another breath then spoke slowly, as if he had to concentrate.

"Before I left, I looked over at a wall and saw D-I-S-M-A-S written in mud. Below the name was some of the carpenter's blood. I could smell flowers. I think he left a sign for whoever came after him to let them know he was still alive. I don't think he killed the trigger man. There were no footprints or signs of struggle anywhere except where the trigger man dropped and died from the snakebite. The doctor said the venom's neurotoxins would have killed him by asphyxiation or heart failure relatively quickly."

Jar Jar paused, almost out of breath from the recollection. "Fast forward a few days later, when school started back up. The tribal leaders came out to watch and make sure it was safe. We had security everywhere. Nobody moved within a five-mile radius without us knowing about it."

Jar Jar grinned with wide eyes. "A couple of kids claimed they'd found a wounded man in a cave and their mother and father were taking care of him."

"The carpenter," Peaches said.

"Exactly. Sarge wanted to find the man to talk to him. The kids refused to tell us where he was. Sarge was pissed. The tribal leaders said it was their duty to protect him; they knew about him too. They knew if we started talking about him over the radios, the enemy would be listening. They were right, because we started hearing old Lurch groaning over the radio that night."

Peaches looked at Barnabas to explain. "There was this insurgent who would come on the radio sometimes. Moaned and groaned like that character Lurch on The Addams Family. We figured he was some kind of big boss."

"The next day, I had the interpreter ask the kids to ask the man in the cave for his name," Jar Jar said. "And Sarge demanded that they ask the carpenter for the name of the man that moaned on the radio, thinking he would know."

"Lurch wanted the carpenter dead," Peaches said, looking at Barnabas to clue him in.

"The kids came back the next day. They said the carpenter's name was Dismas. The moaning man, Lurch, was named Gestas. The day after they talked to the carpenter, the kids said he left the cave. That was right about the same time you left Afghanistan. I think they took you to a hospital in Germany before you went home."

"Did Lurch, or Gestas, I should say, come back on the radio?" Peaches asked.

"No, dead silent. We haven't heard a thing since he said, 'Die, Joseph, die,' the night before the blast. I think the carpenter wanted to let Lurch know he's alive. That's why he signed his name."

Peaches hadn't noticed that Merene was standing behind him. She caught most of Jar Jar's story. He also hadn't noticed when Barnabas got up and left the table.

Dismas. Merene finally remembered why that name sounded so familiar. She had heard Barnabas say it as he stood over Diz's lifeless body before the dog came back to life after the tractor accident.

After a while, Merene made her way to the sanctuary from the fellowship hall to make sure the lights were off before they locked up to head home. Inside, she saw Barnabas with his hands folded and his head bowed in the darkness.

She found a spot to his right and rested on the kneeling pads in front of the altar. She put an arm around the man as he prayed.

# CHAPTER SIXTY-FIVE

The following day, when Barnabas, Merene, Kenneth, and Sharyn were there for lunch, the staff at the City came to their table to pay their respects with deference as the Sunday lunch rush faded.

"So glad to see you, Mr. Hassan," Rex, the restaurant's manager, said. "You haven't aged a bit."

Barnabas, as was typical, lowered his head in silence, uncomfortable with compliments and attention.

"Oh, Rexy," Kenneth said, shaking his head. "I spend enough money here to pay the mortgage, and you ain't ever said a word about my good looks." He smiled when he finished speaking, waiting for the jab to come.

"Oh, Kenneth," Rex said, rubbing the old man's shoulders. "My momma taught me not to lie."

The table broke into laughter.

"Mr. Hassan," Rex asked, "where's Diz? I've never seen you without him."

Merene saw the faintest flash of worry cross Mr. Hassan's face at the mention of Diz. Sharyn saw it too.

"He ran off a while ago. I suppose he'll come back when he's hungry enough," Barnabas said.

"I suppose I'll come back, too, when I'm hungry enough," Kenneth said to Rex.

Sharyn reached across the table and placed her hand near Barnabas's place setting like a mother correcting a child who'd acted up. "Barnabas, he'll come back when he's good and well ready." She touched the fingertips of the hand she had placed in front of Barnabas to her chest. "I can feel it right here."

Barnabas sat stone-faced, like a child who had been scolded.

Kenneth abruptly changed the topic once Peaches came in and sat down. "Well, college boy, how's it going? Is Merene doing your homework for you?"

Peaches and Merene had started the fall semester at Truman State University as biology majors on the pre-medicine track. They were on pace to finish in a couple of years. They had also started volunteering together at the medical center in Kirksville to bolster their résumés for medical school applications in the future.

"The classes are good," Peaches said. "Except for one that I can't really get into."

"Basket weaving?" Kenneth asked. He was trying hard not to laugh at his own joke. He finally relented, wheezing and sputtering like a car that wouldn't start.

"I guess I'd rather be in the lab than reading about ancient civilizations," Peaches said.

"What's the name of the class?" Kenneth asked. "Just in case I'm ever on a TV game show."

"Anthropology," Merene said. "I love it. It's so fascinating."

"Anthro-what?"

"Anthropology," Barnabas said. "The scientific study of humanity."

"Now you've got too many big words for my liking there," Kenneth said, joking.

"Anthropology has four parts: archaeology, linguistics, physical anthropology, and cultural anthropology," Merene said. "Stones, tones, bones, and thrones. That's the easiest way to remember it."

"I like that. Why use fancy words when simpler ones work just fine?" Kenneth asked.

"Parsimony," Peaches said.

"Why are you messing up our nice conversation with your big words again?" Kenneth asked.

"It means simplest is best," Peaches said.

"Amen."

"It's not that bad, I guess," Peaches said. "We have to read a lot and listen to lectures, which, honestly, are pretty interesting. There's a big paper due at the end of the semester. I'm sure I'll survive."

"I already picked a topic for my paper," Merene said. "Glastonbury. The town in England, not the convenience store. I'll need to talk to you, Barnabas."

"I made many happy memories there," Barnabas said. "Many."

They waited for the check, but it didn't come. Lunch was on the house. As they got up to leave, Merene nudged Kenneth.

"You still owe me some pictures, sir."

Kenneth suddenly looked serious. "I've got a few from the old days. You would definitely enjoy them."

"I'm putting together a scrapbook for the Miners' Ball in a few months," Merene said to Peaches. "It was amazing last year. You'll love it."

"I'm sure I will. As long as I don't have to dance."

After leaving the City, Kenneth pulled into the campus of Truman State University, a short drive from the restaurant. Peaches hopped out of the truck in running shorts and a cutoff T-shirt. He had changed at the restaurant after they finished eating. Sharyn had left the restaurant with Barnabas.

"Don't study too hard," Merene said.

"I've got to catch up on my reading. Not all of us can do our homework on the clock," Peaches said with a wink. "I'll meet you at the market around closing time."

Peaches pecked Merene on the cheek as he headed to the library. When he finished, he would get some exercise with a run back to Novinger.

"Where's my kiss?" Kenneth asked. He wheezed as he laughed at himself.

It was a hilly jaunt of about ten miles from the campus to the Glastonbury Market. It would take Peaches an hour and some change to jog back. He had arranged his notes in a pile and given them to a library attendant when he'd finished studying. He would pick the papers up the following day, when he was back for class.

It was a perfect Sunday afternoon in northeast Missouri. A gentle breeze was at his back. A man watched him as he ran and followed him from a distance.

As Peaches loped out of town, he was alone. His only company was the pavement of the road ahead as his running shoes tapped in cadence, one step after another. But Peaches felt like he was being watched, a feeling he hadn't had since Afghanistan. Then a wicked smell hit him. An awful, putrid, rotting smell. He stopped momentarily to make sure he hadn't stepped in something.

His shoes were spotless, save for a few random flecks of dust, which he brushed off with the back of his hand. The smell lingered. He looked in the sky, expecting to see vultures circling over some nearby roadkill. Nothing.

Try as he might, he couldn't outrun the awful essence. The stench followed him, pervading his body, choking his breath. Instead of a leisurely jog, he raced to Novinger as fast as he could.

"You're early," Merene said as Peaches opened the jingling door to the market. "Are you feeling all right? You look like you've just seen a ghost."

"This godawful smell followed me the whole way from Kirksville," Peaches said.

Merene reached into one of the coolers and handed him a Gatorade.

"I guess I'll close now," she said. "Take it easy for a minute."

Peaches sipped from the bottle, which was too cold to chug. He leaned back in a chair behind the cash register as Merene counted and balanced her drawer.

"You ready?"

Peaches moved slowly as they headed for her car, parked out back. Merene paused to lock the back door.

"Kenneth and Sharyn want us to come over tomorrow night. He wants to show us his old pictures. Barnabas is coming over too. I'm opening the market tomorrow morning before class, so you'll have to drive to school on your own."

When they got to his house, Peaches climbed out of the car and spoke to her through the rolled-down window. "I love you, Merene."

She was caught off guard. They weren't usually sentimental. "I might love you if you take a shower!"

The loose gravel crackled under her tires as she drove away.

Before Peaches went into the house, he decided to head to his father's shop. He opened the door and flipped on the light. It was exactly as he had remembered it. His dad's things were organized like they had been when he left for the army. He flipped off the light, shut the door, and made his way toward the house, where he could see from the window his mother was watching TV inside.

Before he opened the front door, he caught the faintest scent of perfume. He recognized the scent from Afghanistan. He closed his eyes for a moment and saw the carpenter's face. "Phantosmia," he said. The doctor at Walter Reed Medical Center had told him that the head injury he suffered in the blast might cause olfactory hallucinations. He hadn't experienced anything of the sort until now.

He breathed through his nose. Nothing but fresh, clean Missouri air filled his lungs. His mind was finished playing tricks on him.

# CHAPTER SIXTY-SIX

"This reminds me of my favorite subject in school," Kenneth said, as he finished eating the cornbread and beans Sharyn had prepared for everyone. "Show and tell."

"Let's see what you have there, Kenneth," Barnabas said.

Kenneth produced an old box of photographs. They had to have been really old, based on their musty, stale scent alone. Sharyn cleared the table for the coming presentation. Kenneth looked at the photographs carefully, like a poker player examining the cards in a hand.

"Who is that?" he said, sliding a photograph gently toward Peaches and Merene.

"Mr. Seeley! I never imagined him being a young man. All I remember was his proud reminder that church was over before he gave us cookies," Merene said. The back of the photograph read "W. Seeley, 19—." The date was smudged.

"When was this taken?" Peaches asked.

Kenneth looked at Barnabas.

"Sometime during the Depression, if I had to guess," Barnabas said.

Kenneth looked at the next photograph carefully. Merene couldn't tell if he was about to laugh or cry.

"Mother and dad," he said.

The back of the photograph read "Arthur and Clara Love." There was no date. Kenneth's father was posed in a wide stance. His mother's chin was turned downward, as if shying away from the camera.

"They looked so happy," Merene said.

"Two of the finest people I've ever met," Barnabas said. "The salt of the earth."

The next picture wasn't as clear as the others. "Another," Kenneth said.

"That's your dad," Merene said. "But what's he holding?"

"A dog," Barnabas said.

"I can see it now," Peaches said. "A little lapdog."

Barnabas gazed at Kenneth.

"What's wrong?" Merene asked.

"Nothing. Just a lot of memories of good friends I miss," Barnabas said. "Old age gets lonely when your friends leave you behind."

"Read the back of this one first," Kenneth said.

Merene did as she was told. Peaches, interested, looked over her shoulder. It read "J. O. Armati—Glastonbury Mining Company" in cursive so neat and clean it looked like calligraphy.

"Turn it over," Kenneth said.

She did.

The man, Joseph Armati, was holding a little dog, whose head was lowered. He wore a porkpie hat like Barnabas's. Merene and Peaches stared so intently at the photograph that they hadn't noticed Barnabas had put on his porkpie hat.

"Whoa!" Merene yelped. "You scared me!"

Peaches looked at Barnabas and again at the photograph. The dog had a black circle on the top of his head, like Diz's. "Does that say 1884?" Peaches asked.

"It does," Barnabas said.

"This is the owner of the Glastonbury Mining Company? Joseph Armati? If I didn't know any better, I'd say that's you, Barnabas."

"You would be right," Barnabas said. "Joseph Armati opened the Glastonbury Mining Company in Novinger in 1884."

Merene looked up, surprised. She glanced over at Sharyn, who had prepared tea for everyone. She had that wry, faint wrinkle of a smile on her face.

The man in the photograph looked to be in his forties, though it was hard to age people from bygone eras.

"I don't understand," Merene said.

Sharyn laughed.

"The dog is a spitting image of Diz," Peaches said. "It has the same black spot on its head."

Barnabas sipped his tea slowly. The steam rose from his mug as he drank.

"What year did Joseph Armati die?" Merene asked. "I know he's not buried here in town. Did he go back to England?"

"We stayed," Barnabas said.

"What do you mean 'we'? I don't get it."

Barnabas took off his hat. "My name is Joseph," he said. He pointed at Diz in the picture. "My friend there is Dismas."

"You mean to tell me you're Joseph Armati?" Peaches said.

Sharyn laughed.

"Yes," Barnabas said. "Yes and no."

"That would make you, like, one hundred and fifty years old!" Merene said, nearly shouting.

"It would," Barnabas said. "If Joseph Armati were a real person."

Peaches squeezed Merene's hand and smiled.

Barnabas stood up. He grabbed a long stick leaning in the corner of the kitchen that no one had paid any attention to until then.

"Let's take a walk. I'd like to show you my private study."

"You go ahead," Kenneth said. "My hips and knees can't keep up with you youngsters and those stairs." He had gathered the photographs of his mother and father into a pile to look through again.

Peaches and Barnabas walked side by side across the field to the entrance of the old Glastonbury Mine. Peaches struggled to keep up with the man, whose stride was long and quick. Merene and Sharyn followed.

Merene saw now that Barnabas's measured steps and slow movements were nothing but a show. He moved naturally like a healthy younger man.

Barnabas stood by the hawthorns clustered along the side of the main entrance. He turned to his companions and winked. He raised the walking stick out in front of his body. He tapped the hawthorns. They immediately flowered.

Merene covered her mouth. Peaches laughed and held her tight.

"Come," Barnabas said.

Behind the flowering trees lay a short, narrow path that dead-ended into a giant slab of stone.

Sharyn stopped to admire the fresh hawthorn blooms. She closed her eyes to enjoy their perfume.

Barnabas tapped the stone with the walking stick. It rolled away, uncovering a staired pathway dropping down deep into the mine.

Peaches held Merene's hand as they followed Barnabas. Just as soon as Sharyn had cleared the threshold of the entrance, the huge stone rolled back into place. The mine was dim but not completely dark. A faint glow illuminated their steps. The two stood in what could be considered an atrium. Peaches looked up at the vaulted ceilings like a kid watching a Fourth of July fireworks display.

"What do you think?" Sharyn said. Peaches had never been there, though he had seen a library in the mine a long time ago. Nothing was as wonderful as this space. It might as well have been a museum. Peaches found a book protected by a clear case.

"Is this what I think it is?" Peaches asked.

"That might depend on what you think it is," Barnabas said.

"A Gutenberg Bible? An actual Gutenberg Bible? That's got to be four hundred years old!"

"A little older, maybe. It was printed in the 1450s, if memory serves me right. I remember buying it brand-new."

Next to the Gutenberg Bible was a first edition of Isaac Newton's Principia. "1687," Barnabas said, unsolicited. "Newton was brilliant. Absolutely brilliant."

Merene had wandered a bit, admiring tapestries, paintings, and an assortment of wall hangings from around the world. "This is better than any museum in Saint Louis," she said. "Maybe even better than Chicago or New York City." She wiped tears from her eyes. Happy tears.

"I've had a lot of time to collect. Thankfully, I have a wonderful archivist to help me," Barnabas said, looking at Sharyn.

Sharyn walked down a hall. "Come here," she said, motioning for Merene and Peaches.

Around a corner was a small room.

"A chapel?" Merene asked.

The room was cool and dry. It smelled sweetly of flowers, a scent Peaches immediately recognized. The room held a plain table with a plain wooden cross on it. It looked very old.

"Dismas," Peaches said. "Is he here?"

Barnabas kneeled at the altar, bowing his head to pray. Instinctively, Merene joined him. She closed her eyes and put an arm around Barnabas. Peaches and Sharyn joined them.

When they opened their eyes, the small wooden cross on the table was draped in a cream garment. A plain pottery cup rested in front of it. The four sat back on a small pew with a plush cushion. Peaches ran his hand over the smooth olive wood.

Barnabas broke the still silence. "Peace. Peace be with you."

Merene was the only one to respond. "And also with you."

Barnabas gazed at the little table with a thousand-yard stare. "My real name is Joseph. I come from Arimathea, an area in Judea. My life, really, was unimportant until the day he was crucified. I begged Caiaphas for his body, to give him a proper burial. That was the cloth I wrapped him in. The cup was the one he shared with his disciples before he was taken."

Peaches began to whimper. "I remember as a kid believing that you were an angel. This is even better."

Merene held his hand.

Barnabas looked over at Sharyn with misty eyes. "The cup and the staff have stayed with me as I've wandered across the world, continuing the work of Jesus of Nazareth. I long for the day I meet him again."

He turned his face to Peaches. Merene rested her head on Sharyn's shoulder.

"Two thieves were nailed next to Jesus. When I went to gather his body, they were both alive. Dismas, on the cross, begged for forgiveness.

His heart was changed. Jesus told him that he would join him in paradise that day. I heard it with my own two ears. I can't explain how or why, but Dismas went to heaven and was sent back. The fragrance, the scent of the lilies of paradise, has remained with him. He was with you in Afghanistan."

"I know he was. I knew it was him!" Peaches said.

"Barnabas," Merene said. "Or Joseph. I've known you my entire life, and now I don't know what to call you! If Dismas turned into a dog, are you about to tell me that you can turn into a house cat?"

Sharyn hooted. Her laughs filled the high vaults of the underground labyrinth.

"There are many things I can't explain, though I'd like to know myself," Barnabas said. "But the answer is no. I've been stuck in this body since Christ's death, though I haven't aged. Dismas was given the bodily form of a dog by a man in dazzling white when we sailed for Glastonbury."

"An angel?" Merene asked.

"An angel," he said. "From time to time, Dismas becomes a man again. But you'd be surprised how useful having four legs rather than two can be."

"What about Gestas?" Peaches asked. "What happened to him?"

Barnabas drew a long, slow breath. "He's out there somewhere. Dismas and I have traveled throughout the centuries to build up and do good. Gestas has done the opposite—stealing, destroying, killing."

"Centuries," Merene said. "It's so strange to hear someone say that."

"Gestas hates Dismas more than anyone. Dismas changed when he was dying next to Christ… and when he did, he was no longer afraid of Gestas. I think that deep down, Gestas knows he'll have to answer for all the pain and suffering he has caused someday."

"Has he tried to kill you over the years?" Peaches asked.

"In a way. He knows we have a great protector, that our bodies are safe. Gestas is consumed by hatred. He has no purpose except to destroy. The man in white, the angel, came to me again not long ago. I hadn't heard from him in years."

"Why did Diz die, then?" Merene asked. "I saw him killed by that tractor wheel!"

"The cup is miraculous. It heals." Barnabas froze for a moment in thought. "My time here in Novinger is nearing an end."

This revelation caught Sharyn's attention.

Barnabas tapped the walking stick. "It'll be time to move on soon."

"What about Dismas?" Peaches said. "I don't understand."

Barnabas hung his head. "Dismas will deal with Gestas. When he finishes the work set before him, the angel told me, he'll return to paradise. For good."

"What do you mean?" Peaches said.

Barnabas looked down. "Dismas will leave," he said. "And I will remain. I've left a thousand places in my lifetime. Leaving this place might be the hardest yet. I'll be alone this time, back to wandering."

"Why can't you stay with us?" Peaches asked.

Barnabas smiled. "I don't make the rules. I just follow them. There's somewhere else where I'm needed."

Merene had regained her composure. She turned to Peaches. "If an angel appeared to you and told you to do something, would you argue?"

The four talked for hours, punctuated by intermittent episodes of laughter or tears. When they left, Sharyn plucked a hawthorn flower and placed it in Merene's hair.

"Get some sleep, young 'un," she said as she tucked the bloom gently to the top of her head. "When you wake up, this will remind you that you weren't dreaming."

In the morning, the flower rested on her pillow when Merene woke up. It smelled even more beautiful than she remembered.

# CHAPTER SIXTY-SEVEN

"You sure know how to party," Peaches said to Merene as they made their way to an auditorium on campus days later. "A guest lecture on Myths and Legends in Antiquity is my idea of a slammin' Friday night."

"Quit your whining," Merene said. "It'll be interesting, and we get extra credit for being here. We can leave a little early. I have to go to the market for a couple of hours and then close."

A mousy man approached the lectern. "Oh, hello," the speaker said. "I don't know if I should be humbled by your presence or disappointed that you don't have better things to do with your evening."

A bright spotlight revealed the speaker's pallor and the incredibly thick lenses of his glasses.

"I actually wanted to wear a T-shirt and jeans, but I thought better of it." He rubbed the elbow patches on the blazer he wore, which was probably twice as old as any of the students in the room. "A professor of antiquities needs to look the part."

"He's funny," Peaches whispered to Merene.

"I guess I forgot to introduce myself," the professor said. "How rude. I'm Dr. Johan Dries, visiting professor of Epigraphical and Paleographical Studies. Anyone interested in anthropology? Antiquities? Research? Woeful, virtuous suffering?"

A few hands rose in the audience. He pointed at his face as he sported a cheesy grin. "Splendid! Then this is what you have to look forward to. Take a hard look at me. You could end up just like this!"

The crowd chuckled.

"Anthropology is fascinating. My life has been richer and more beautiful because of it. Before I continue to ramble on, which is basically what professors do for a living, I want to thank our generous sponsor, Mr. Barnabas Hassan, who paid for my travel and for this entire lecture series. He was unable to join us this evening. I understand Mr. Hassan is well up in age, which makes me like him all the more. This might surprise you, but I really like old stuff."

The crowd laughed again.

"Just a warning to prepare yourselves. I'm going to sing classic rock lyrics randomly. I may tell some jokes. I find myself hilarious. Most old men do. When we're finished, if anyone is still awake, I'll answer questions."

Dr. Dries looked up at the ceiling and whipped his head back, further disheveling his already disheveled hair. He feigned an intense and dramatic air-guitar solo, using his microphone as a prop. The brief performance drew enthusiastic applause. Then he began the lecture.

Hours later, Merene leaned over to Peaches and whispered, "We've got to go. It's almost nine."

Peaches couldn't believe that much time had flown by. Dr. Dries was mesmerizing and entertaining, a fountain of knowledge. Merene nudged Peaches.

"Let me ask a question," he said. "And then we'll head out." Peaches raised his hand.

"Yes, sir," Dr. Dries said. "I feel like I should buy you a beer for staying this long."

"What do legends say about Joseph of Arimathea?" Peaches asked.

The air guitar made a triumphant encore with renewed applause. "It's an interesting and specific question. Legends and lore say Joseph of Arimathea traveled to Glastonbury, England, to bring Christianity to Britannia. Our benefactor, Barnabas Hassan, is from Glastonbury, from what I understand. We have corresponded often. He has a wealth of knowledge on this particular topic.

"In the Middle Ages, written lore identified Joseph of Arimathea as the keeper of the Holy Grail, the cup Christ shared with his disciples at the Last Supper. This is in sharp contrast to what most people think, that some other English guy named Monty Python has the Holy Grail. During the thirteenth century, a Latin chronicle written by British monks recorded a legend that the fate of Joseph of Arimathea was to walk the earth until the Second Coming of Christ.

"Good question, sir. My beer offer still stands."

As they slipped out the back quietly, Peaches froze near the exit.

"What's wrong?" Merene asked.

Peaches's nose wrinkled. That awful smell had returned. The rotten, something-died smell. "Do you smell anything?" he said.

"Not really," Merene said.

Peaches shrugged. "Phantosmia. Olfactory hallucinations. I swear I smell something dead in here."

"It's all in your head, man." Merene pecked him on the cheek and squeezed his hand as they left the auditorium together.

A man who'd been sitting alone, wearing sunglasses and a black hooded sweatshirt, left and followed not far behind them. He reeked of rotting flesh.

Dark storm clouds loomed in the sky as Peaches and Merene made it to the parking lot.

"It looks creepy," Merene said. "Like the world is going to end."

Peaches sang the last verse of the classic rock song that had been playing on the car radio when they started the engine. Merene had quickly turned off the radio so she could concentrate on driving in the bad weather.

"If the world is ending, at least we'll die together, my love," Peaches said. "How romantic."

"I'd like to romantically reach over and slap you, but unfortunately, I can't do that right now." Her knuckles whitened as she maintained a death grip on the steering wheel. They drove slowly the whole way to Novinger.

She shook her head as they pulled around behind the Glastonbury Market. The parking lot out front was full.

"Storms are always good for sales. People can't be without their beer, cigarettes, and Mountain Dew." Merene surveyed the gravel of the parking lot, plotting out the fewest moves to hop inside the back door without getting soaked. "Bye!" she said, winking at Peaches.

He opened his door to find a lake forming in a pothole the hard rains had exacerbated. He climbed across the seat to step out on the driver's side instead, where Merene had made a hasty exit moments before. Out of the corner of his eye, he saw a beat-up old car with one headlight pull in. Its driver looked over in his direction.

"You must be high, man," Peaches said. "Sunglasses in a rainstorm. Really?"

The driver probably hadn't seen the light of day for a long time. Sadly, the market was frequented by a steady stream of addicts who surfaced only once or twice a week for food and drinks in between benders.

Peaches raised his chin to acknowledge the driver, who had parked and was staring at him.

The moment Peaches opened the car door, a cloudburst dumped buckets of rain, soaking him. Merene snickered as Peaches's wet shoes squished and squeaked while he walked inside through the store's back door.

The rush of customers had almost died down. A handful of people stood in line waiting as Merene checked them out with surgical precision. "Be careful out there," she told customers as they left.

A rolling wheel on the bright-yellow mop bucket screeched as Peaches dragged it down each aisle, sopping up the outlines of soggy footprints. Merene looked over at him and mouthed a thank-you from across the room. He blew her a playful kiss and returned to the task. An unexpected twinge of warmth spread across her neck and shoulders. Little things like that were what made her love Peaches. He was thoughtful.

"Damn it," Peaches said, hauling the mop and bucket back to the closet. "I forgot my backpack in the car."

"Don't worry about it," Merene said. "I'm not going to stay around much longer." She looked around at the shelves and coolers, counting more bare spots than could be recorded on both hands. "We're pretty well wiped out."

But Peaches ducked out the back. The man wearing sunglasses sat in the parking lot, exactly as he had been when Peaches went in the first time. Peaches grabbed his bag from the car and went back inside.

A huge flash of lightning coursed through the night sky, followed by an ear-splitting rumble of thunder. The lights inside the store went out for several moments. When they returned, Peaches saw the man wearing sunglasses in the back of the store. He hadn't heard or seen him enter.

"Sir, we're going to close soon," Merene said. "I'm sorry if we don't have what you're looking for at the moment."

The man toddled unsteadily, like a baby.

"I need to call Barnabas," Merene said, "to see if he needs anything from here before we head back."

The man paused and turned his head toward the register.

"Can I help you, sir?" Peaches asked. He had barely finished speaking when the smell hit him—the same reeking, rotten smell from the auditorium. Peaches coughed into the corner of his elbow, trying to be polite. The stench was overwhelming.

Merene came from the backroom. "Phone's dead," she said. "The storm must've knocked it out."

The shelves rattled as another clap of thunder sounded. As she turned toward the corner where Peaches was standing, she caught a whiff of the smell. Peaches saw her nose wrinkle. Her lips rose in protest.

"What is that smell?" she whispered to him.

Lightning flashed. The lights cut out. The two could barely see the outline of the man in the darkness, since the lightning provided intermittent illumination.

"Sir, just take what you need. We can settle up later."

The man didn't reply.

The stench grew stronger.

Merene thought she was going to vomit. She popped the foil on the back of a pack of chewing gum and found a few pieces for herself and for Peaches. But not even the minty gum could hide the overpowering odor.

The lights flickered back on at what seemed to be half strength. The store was suspended in an eerie partial light.

"Sir, it's nasty out there. Please just head on home."

He inched forward, toward the counter. The contrast of his pale skin against his dark-black hooded sweatshirt was stark. A thick black ringlet of his hair nestled on top of the black sunglasses.

Peaches grabbed Merene's hand when he saw the man's hair move on its own, revealing the tapered tail of a snake. "Sir, we're closing up now," Peaches said. His voice cracked a bit. "You can go. No need to pay." He chomped hard on the chewing gum with his mouth open, trying to blow wafts of mint to his nostrils for relief from the rottenness.

The man stopped a few feet from the counter and stood still. The lights returned to full strength and then some. They seemed to burn twice as brightly as they should have. They hummed like the unnerving buzz of a dentist's drill.

"Where is he?" the man groaned. He raised a pistol, pointing it directly at Merene. She grabbed the side of Peaches's wet pants.

Peaches spoke slowly and clearly. "There's no one else here, sir. Put the gun down."

The back door closed after another explosion of thunder, startling Merene. "Jesus!" she shouted.

The three heard footsteps.

"He's not here," a familiar voice said. "Gestas, leave these kids alone. They're innocent."

Peaches swallowed. Gestas was Lurch, the moaning man on the radio in Afghanistan. Gestas, the killer of the innocent. Gestas, the man who sent Batman to his death. Gestas, the man who rebuked Christ on the cross.

"Joseph," the man said. "It's been a long time." He pulled his hood off, revealing long black hair.

Barnabas Hassan stood like a statue, staring at the man.

With his left hand, Gestas removed his black sunglasses. The sunglasses had covered gaping black holes in his skull where eyes should have been. The small flaring head of a black cobra slid out from the holes into the light. Its forked tongue flickered.

Merene drew a long, deep breath. Peaches squeezed her hand.

The man pointed the gun at Barnabas.

"Am I supposed to be afraid, Gestas?" Barnabas asked.

Gestas pointed the gun back at Merene.

The lights hummed louder than ever. Bulbs began to pop and shatter. One, two, three. The store grew darker with each tiny explosion.

Then the familiar perfume found his nostrils—Peaches smelled Dismas before he saw him. He closed his eyes.

"Dismas," he whispered to Merene. "He's here."

In the back of the store stood Dismas. The carpenter. Sweat glistened on his brow. His dark hair met his shoulders. He had a long, straight face. His eyes were clear and bright, almost as bright as the dazzling white tunic he wore. "Gestas," Dismas said. "Your time's up."

Peaches could see he was holding Barnabas's staff above his head.

With his back turned to Dismas, Gestas scoffed. "Wait your turn, boy. I'll get to you next."

Peaches let go of Merene's hand as he heard Gestas click the pistol's trigger. "No!" Peaches yelled.

He jumped in front of Merene as the last remaining light bulb burst.

Merene saw a flicker of lightning flash from the staff. It filled the blackened room with a blinding, white-hot intensity. Merene shielded her eyes. Peaches's body slumped to the floor as the store erupted into flames. Her hands shook as they were soaked by the blood spurting from Peaches's body. She pressed two fingers to his neck and searched for a pulse. It soon faded to nothing.

Merene collapsed, clutching Peaches. She watched Barnabas and Dismas in a daze. They carried her and Peaches out behind the store. Dismas raised the staff above his head. The night sky above the back porch cleared. The rain-soaked ground dried instantly.

Merene didn't know what to think. She thought she might be dead like Peaches, who they had propped up in a sitting position in a corner.

Dismas passed the staff to Barnabas. "This is goodbye, old friend," he said.

Barnabas held the back of the man's head like a parent consoling a frightened child. "Peace," Barnabas said. "Peace be with you."

Dismas reached into the pocket of his loose white shirt. He handed the cup from Barnabas's private altar to him. "God be with you, Joseph," Dismas said. "God be with you till we meet again."

He turned from Barnabas and took a step forward. He raised his hands into the air, holding them like a child waiting to be picked up by a parent.

A bolt of lightning struck him without a sound.

Merene blinked. Dismas was gone.

"What is happening?" she screamed.

She sobbed and covered her face with her hands. She looked over at Peaches, who sat awkwardly as if he had fallen asleep in a car. The bullet he took for her had pierced the middle of his chest. He probably hadn't felt a thing.

Barnabas sat down next to Merene. He placed the cup on the ground. When Merene looked at it, she saw the cup had filled with what smelled like sweet wine.

"Merene."

Barnabas had tears in his eyes. She felt the wetness of his cheeks as he hugged her tightly.

The fire in the store belched and crackled. Glass shattered.

Kneeling before Peaches, Barnabas raised his hands in the air, his wrists touching as if they were fastened together. He reached for the cup, holding it steady with both hands. He dabbed a finger in it and ran a wine-soaked thumb over Peaches's blanched lips. "Drink," he said.

He brought the cup to Peaches's mouth.

# CHAPTER SIXTY-EIGHT

"Come this way," the man Dismas said. "They've been waiting for you."

It was sunny and warm. The scent of flowers filled the air with a pleasant freshness. A gentle breeze fluttered.

Peaches extended his arms out like wings, stretching like one did when waking up from a satisfying nap. He felt wonderful. Lighter than air.

Dismas bounded ahead to the top of a hill in the distance, his long hair blowing back in the wind. A small gathering of people surrounded him. He motioned for Peaches to follow.

It might have been a half mile away. He couldn't tell. He heard a faint chant. "Run, Peaches, run!"

He walked.

"Run, Peaches, run!"

His walk became a jog. His jog became a run. His feet flew so fast he felt like he was flying.

"Run, Peaches, run!" the voices said. He ran faster. They yelled louder. "Run, Peaches, run!"

He realized he wasn't out of breath, nor was he straining in any way. He looked to his left. A sea of friendly faces waved and cheered. A kindly man caught his attention, a face that seemed familiar.

It was Kenneth's father, Arthur Love! His wife, Clara, stood next to him, clapping. Next to her was Willie Seeley, the young man they had taken in from the orphan train when Kenneth was a child.

"Run, Peaches, run!" they cheered. Willie clapped wildly. He gave Peaches a thumbs-up.

"Peaches!" A woman's voice cut through the din as he sprinted.

Over his right shoulder, he saw Teresa Cory. If he had breath, the sight of her would have taken it away. She was beautiful; her skin glowed with an angelic radiance. She was happy. He had never seen her so happy. She saw him slow his pace. She shook her head as she pointed at the top of the hill.

"Run, Peaches, run!" she said.

The other faces in the crowd were many and familiar. He wanted desperately to stop to talk to and hug each and every person gathered there, but they wouldn't let him.

"Run, Peaches, run!" they said, urging him onward to the top of the hill.

Up ahead, Dismas spoke with a man who, if he didn't know better, Peaches would have sworn was Peaches himself.

"Dad?" Peaches said.

The man heard him and nodded.

"Dad!" Peaches shouted, quickening his pace. "I'm coming!"

There were kids next to the men.

"Brady!" he screamed. "Brady!"

Brady looked tall and strong, his head full of hair like it had been before the cancer stole it. "Run, Peaches, run!" Brady said.

A boy crouched behind Brady. He jumped out in front of him.

"Batman!" Peaches said. "I'm coming!"

Batman turned around and extended his hand behind him where Peaches couldn't yet see. His sister Gabina emerged and stood next to the boys.

"Run, Peaches, run!" they said.

Peaches reached the top of the hill and looked at Dismas in shock. He wanted to cry but couldn't.

"There are no tears in heaven," Dismas said.

Peaches's dad came toward him. "Son, I'm so proud of you! I'm so proud of you! Don't ever forget that."

He hugged Peaches. Peaches couldn't remember the last time his father had done such a thing.

Brady, Batman, and Gabina joined in.

"They need you at home," Brady said. "It's not your time to be here with us."

"We'll be waiting for you," Batman said.

Peaches stood still until Gabina spoke. The deaf girl spoke! "You and Merene are going to be doctors together, healing people all over the world."

Brady raised his eyebrows as he revealed an I-told-you-so grin.

"When you have children someday, you go easy on my grandkids," Peaches's father said. "You understand?"

"It's time for you to go," Dismas said. "God be with you till we meet again, friend."

The crowd chanted "Run, Peaches, run," interrupted only by the joyous singsong of laughter.

Peaches looked at Dismas.

"Merene needs you," Dismas said.

"Merene," Peaches said.

# CHAPTER SIXTY-NINE

The sweetness tingled his tongue as Peaches licked his moistened lips. He sipped from the cup slowly before cradling it with two hands as he emptied it.

"Are you okay?" Merene asked.

"There's no way I could possibly feel better," Peaches said. He felt warm and relaxed.

His fingers found a hole and shredded fabric in the center of his shirt. He felt his chest. Nothing but smooth, bare skin. Not a spot of blood nor any torn flesh to be found. "What happened?" he asked.

Kenneth and Sharyn pulled up behind the market. They chatted with Barnabas as the conflagration devoured the little store. It was only a matter of time before volunteers from the fire department would be showing up.

Later, sitting in the truck with Peaches and Merene, Sharyn closed her eyes for a moment and breathed through her nose. "You smell like heaven," she said, looking at Peaches. "And you look like hell. Let's get you both home."

Merene ran her hand over his face, feeling a few bumps and scrapes. He had blistered a bit from the heat of the fire. Merene realized she had too. The truck tires skidded as they mashed the wet gravel of the drive leading back to Kenneth and Sharyn's house. The pair fell asleep when they sat down inside.

When they awoke, Barnabas greeted them, sipping tea. Kenneth sat nearby, folding in half slices of square-top wheat bread slathered with peanut butter and dunking them into his hot coffee.

"Where's Dismas?" Peaches asked. He watched Barnabas, who was writing on a notepad as steam climbed from the top of his cup and disappeared.

Barnabas rose to his feet, quick and spry like a young man. He bounced on his heels as he paced around the room, full of nervous energy. "He finished his work here and went home. He finally went home," Barnabas said. "Merene, congratulations are in order. You're the first executive director of the Novinger Community Improvement Foundation."

"What does that mean?" she asked.

"Sharyn can fill you in on the details later. I've set aside enough money to do good in this place forever. You'll officially become the executor of the foundation's trust after you've graduated from medical school, or when you turn thirty years old, whichever comes first." He handed the scrap of notepaper to her, which had a sum written on it.

Peaches peered over her shoulder. "Good God!" he said. The number had an impressive string of zeros.

"God, indeed, is good," Barnabas said. "And you, my friends"—his voice cracked—"so are you."

Kenneth pulled the top off a box that he'd set on the table. Peaches looked inside.

"After the fire went out, I poked around through the ashes. Nothing left but this," Kenneth said. "Must've died from the smoke, but I can't figure out how he got there to begin with or how he didn't burn up in the flames."

"Black desert cobra," Peaches said.

"Gestas won't bother anyone anymore," Barnabas said. He tapped the head of the snake. It turned to dust.

For a long while, they sat at the table together like they had done a thousand times before, talking and laughing. Finally, when he was rising to leave, Barnabas Hassan took up his staff and put on his porkpie hat. The cup and linen were tucked inside a shirt pocket near his heart.

"God be with you till we meet again, my friends." The rambling man opened the front door and looked outside. "Till we meet again."

# EPILOGUE

Dr. Merene Peecher opened the door of the little house she shared with her husband, Dr. Jackson Peecher. It had been willed to the couple as a gift by the estate of Barnabas Hassan after they graduated from medical school and were married. Their past few years together had been kind, though they showed the crow's feet and stray gray hairs that married couples gave one another.

"Be quiet, young 'un," Sharyn said. "My sweet baby is finally sleeping." Sharyn showed her age as well. She still walked on her own but never without the assistance of a cane.

"At least he sleeps for you, because he sure doesn't sleep for me," Merene whispered. She ducked her head inside the nursery, where "Brady Barnabas" was stenciled on the wall above the crib.

Then she came back to the kitchen, where Sharyn was pouring hot water into two cups. Her aged hand tremored slightly.

"Well?" She looked at Merene's belly. "Still Baby No-Name?"

"Baby No-Name is another boy. God help me." She rubbed her stomach as hot tea trickled down her throat. "Patman. Patman Joseph."

"I like the sound of it," Sharyn said. She slipped a letter across the table to Merene.

"What's this?" Merene looked up and noticed that leaning on a chair was Barnabas Hassan's staff. "Oh my God! He's here?" Merene said. "He's really here?"

"You know where to find him," Sharyn said.

Peaches walked through the door just then to find Merene and Sharyn talking.

"Let's go for a walk," Merene said.

"Merene, I've been working for sixteen hours straight at the hospital! I want to see the baby for a minute and go to bed."

Sharyn shook her head. "You men don't learn. Don't ever argue with a pregnant lady."

Merene waddled to the door. She grabbed the staff, catching Peaches's attention.

"Oh my God," Peaches said. "He's here?"

Peaches raced across the field toward the old Glastonbury Mine, looking back at Merene when he realized he had left her far behind.

"I'd run, but Patman Joseph is slowing me down."

"Patman Joseph!" Peaches said, repeating it with emphasis. He ran to his wife and stopped to kiss her like they did in the movies, cupping her face with the palms of both of his hands.

"Now you're slowing me down!" she said.

When they reached the mine, they found the spot where the thicket of hawthorns stood. Their sweet-smelling flowers were in full bloom. The great stone stood locked in place, blocking the entrance.

Merene tapped it with the staff. It rolled away. An almost blinding brightness poured forth.

Together, Merene and Peaches walked into the light.

# ABOUT THE AUTHOR

Gabe Reaume won a countywide writing contest in elementary school and hasn't stopped writing since. Raised in rural Michigan, Gabe eventually moved to Texas to study local government management. He lives in Saginaw, Texas, where he serves as the city manager. He is married to his wife Cori. They have four children who enjoy sports, travel, and of course, reading.

If you're in North Texas, give Gabe a shout. He would enjoy hearing from you. The coffee is waiting!

www.ingramcontent.com/pod-product-compliance
Lightning Source LLC
Chambersburg PA
CBHW030136010826
48973CB00002B/592